The Ides of Tomorrow

The Ides of Tomorrow

Original Science Fiction Tales of Horror

edited by

Terry Carr

Little, Brown and Company

BOSTON TORONTO

FIRST EDITION
T 10/76

Library of Congress Cataloging in Publication Data

Main entry under title:

The ides of tomorrow.

1. Horror tales, American. 2. Horror tales, English. I. Carr, Terry.
PZ1.I18 [PS648.H6] 823'.0876 76–24866
ISBN 0–316–12970–4

Designed by D. Christine Benders

Published simultaneously in Canada
by Little, Brown & Company (Canada) Limited

PRINTED IN THE UNITED STATES OF AMERICA

Contents

The Ides of Tomorrow

Introduction

SINCE THE EARLIEST DAYS of science fiction, writers have been drawn inexorably to describe the fearsome things that may lie in wait for us beyond tomorrow's dawn. When science itself was still in its infancy, Mary Shelley imagined that we might one day learn to create artificial life in the laboratory, and she wrote *Frankenstein*. When scientists speculated that there might be life on other planets, H. G.

Wells wrote *The War of the Worlds.* As governments experimented in controlling the thoughts of citizens, George Orwell wrote *1984*.

The list of science fiction's warnings about the future continues throughout the era of pulp magazines, right up to today: *Who Goes There?* by John W. Campbell, *The Weapon* by Fredric Brown, *Born of Man and Woman* by Richard Matheson, *I Have No Mouth, and I Must Scream* by Harlan Ellison. These are powerful stories, memorable stories, and the list grows longer every day.

The more we learn about our universe, the more we find that is still a mystery to us — and the unknown is always a trigger for fear.

Here is an anthology of new science fiction horror stories, written by acknowledged masters of the genre as well as by comparative newcomers. In their range of themes they express much of what we fear about the direction our world is taking. They are warnings — not of what *will* happen, but of what we think *might* happen.

Science fiction doesn't predict the future; it only guesses at it. Sometimes its stories later prove to have struck startlingly close to the truth, but they're in the minority.

I hope none of the stories here will ever join that tragic minority.

Terry Carr
February, 1976

Recent breakthroughs in the field of organ transplants have brought new hope and even new life to many people — but every ability our science gives us can be perverted by those with great power and few scruples. What if a mutation were to produce a few fortunate people born with eyes that could see in a new way: shapes within shapes, colors that have never been? How the rest of us would envy those people! . . . and how inevitably that envy could turn to covetousness if a method were discovered to transplant their eyes into the sockets of jaded sybarites. . . .

Harlan Ellison is a superstar of science fiction, the only writer in the field's history to achieve that status purely on the basis of his short stories. *Seeing*, one of his finest stories to date, shows why: Ellison can generate more impact in a novelette than most sf writers can pack into a two-pound novel.

Seeing

Harlan Ellison

"I remember well the time when the thought of the eye made me cold all over."
Charles Darwin, 1860

"HEY. BERNE. Over there. Way back in that booth . . . see her?"

"Not now. I'm tired. I'm relaxing."

"Jizzus, Berne, take a look at her."

"Grebbie, if you don't synch-out and let me get doused, I swear I'll bounce a shot thimble off your skull."

"Okay, have it like you want it. But they're gray-blue."

"What?"

"Forget it, Berne. You said forget it, so forget it."

"Turn around here, man."

"I'm drinking."

"Listen, snipe, we been out all day looking . . ."

"Then when I tell you something from now on, you gonna *hear* me?"

"I'm sorry, Grebbie. Now come on, man, which one is she?"

"Over there. Pin her?"

"The plaid jumper?"

"No, the one way back in the dark in that booth behind the plaid. She's wearing a kaftan . . . wait'll the lights come around again . . . *there*! Y'pin her? Gray-blue, just like the Doc said he wanted."

"Grebbie, you are one beautiful pronger."

"Yeah, huh?"

"Now just turn around and stop staring at her before she sees you. We'll get her."

"How, Berne? This joint's full up."

"She's gotta move out sometime. She'll go away."

"And we'll be right on her, right, Berne?"

"Grebbie, have another punchup and let me drink."

"Jizzus, man, we're gonna be livin' crystalfine when we get them back to the Doc."

"Grebbie!"

"Okay, Berne, okay. Jizzus, she's got beautiful eyes."

From extreme long shot, establishing; booming down to tight closeup, it looked like this:

Viewed through the fisheye-lens of a Long Drive vessel's stateroom iris, as the ship sank to Earth, the area surrounding the pits and pads and terminal structures of PIX, the Polar Interstellar Exchange port authority terminus, was a doughnut-shaped crazy quilt of rampaging colors. In the doughnut hole center was PIX, slate-gray alloys macroscopically homogenized to ignore the onslaughts of deranged Arctic weather. Around the port was a nomansland of eggshell-white plasteel with shock fibers woven into its surface. Nothing could pass across that dead area without permission. A million flickers of beckoning light erupted every second from the colorful doughnut, as if silent Circes called unendingly for visitors to come find their sources. Down, down, the ship would come and settle into its pit, and the view in the iris would vanish. Then tourists would leave the Long Driver through underground slidewalk tunnels that would carry them into the port authority for clearance and medical checks and baggage inspection.

Tram carts would carry the cleared tourists and returning long-drive crews through underground egress passages to the outlets beyond the nomansland. Security waivers signed, all responsibility for their future safety returned to them, their wit and protective devices built into their clothing the only barriers between them and what lay aboveground, they would be shunted into cages and whisked to the surface.

Then the view reappeared. The doughnut-shaped area around the safe port structures lay sprawled before the newly arrived visitors and returnees from space. Without form or design, the area was scatter-packed with a thousand shops and arcades, hostelries and dives, pleasure palaces and food emporiums. As though they had been wind-thrown anemophilously, each structure grew up side by side with its neighbors. Dark and twisting alleyways careened through from one section to the next. Spitalfields in London and Greenwich Village in old New York — before the Crunch — had grown up this way, like a jungle of hungry plants. And every open doorway had its barker, calling and gesturing, luring the visitors into the maw of unexpected experiences. Demander circuits flashed lights directly into the eyes of passersby, operating off retinal-heat-seeking mechanisms. Psychosound loops kept up an unceasing subliminal howling, each message striving to cap those filling the air around it, struggling to capture the attention of tourists with fat credit accounts. Beneath the ground, machinery labored mightily, the occasional squeal of plasteel signifying that even at top-point efficiency the guts of the area could not keep up with the demands of its economy. Crowds flowed in definite patterns, first this way, then that way, following the tidal pulls of a momentarily overriding loop, a barker's spiel filling an eye-of-the-hurricane silence, a strobing demander suddenly reacting to an overload of power.

The crowds contained prongers, coshmen, fagin brats, pleasure pals, dealers, pickpockets, hustlers, waltzers, pseudomarks, gophers, rowdy-dowdy hijackers, horses, hot slough workers, whores, steerers, blousers of all ages, sheiks, shake artists, kiters, floaters, aliens from three hundred different federations, assassins and, of course, innocent johns, marks, hoosiers, kadodies and tourists ripe for shucking.

Following one such tidal flow of crowd life, down an alley identified on a wall as Poke Way, the view would narrow down to a circular doorway in a green one-storey building. The sign would scream THE ELEGANT. Tightening the angle of observation, moving inside, the place could be seen to be a hard-drinking bar.

At the counter, as the sightline tracked around the murky bar, one could observe two men hunched over their thimbles, drinking steadily and paying attention to nothing but what their credit cards could buy, dumbwaitered up through the counter to their waiting hands. To an experienced visitor to the area, they would be clearly identifiable as "butt'n'ben" prongers: adepts at locating and furnishing to various Knox Shops whatever human parts were currently in demand.

Tracking further right, into the darkness of the private booths, the view would reveal (in the moments when the revolving overhead globes shone into those black spaces) an extremely attractive, but weary-looking, young woman with gray-blue eyes. Moving in for a tight closeup, the view would hold that breathtaking face for long moments, then move in and in on the eyes . . . those remarkable eyes.

All this, all these sights, in the area called WorldsEnd.

Verna tried to erase the memory with the oblivion of drink. Drugs made her sick to her stomach and never accomplished what they were supposed to do. But chigger, and rum and bowl could do it . . . if she downed them in sufficient quantities. Thus far, the level had not been even remotely approached. The alien, and what she had had to do to service him were still fresh in her mind. Right near the surface, like scum. Since she had left the safe house and gone on her own, it had been one disaster after another. And tonight, the slug thing from . . .

She could not remember the name of the world it called its home. Where it lived in a pool of liquid, in a state of what passed for grace only to those who raised other life-forms for food.

She punched up another bowl and then some bread, to dip in the thick liquor. Her stomach was sending her messages of pain.

There had to be a way out. Out of WorldsEnd, out of the trade, out of the poverty and pain that characterized this planet for all but the wealthiest and most powerful. She looked into the bowl and saw it as no one else in The Elegant could have seen it.

The brown, souplike liquor, thick and dotted with lighter lumps of amber. She saw it as a whirlpool, spinning down to a finite point of silver radiance that spun on its own axis, whirling and whirling: a mad eye. A funnel of living brilliance flickering with chill heat that ran back against the spin, surging toward the top of the bowl and forming a barely visible surface tension of coruscating light, a thousand-colored dome of light.

She dipped the bread into the funnel and watched it tear apart like the finest lace. She brought it up, soaking, and ripped off a piece with her fine, white, even teeth — thinking of tearing the flesh of her mother. Sydni, her mother, who had gifted her with this curse, these eyes. This terrible curse that prevented her from seeing the world as it was, as it might have been, as it might be; seeing the world through eyes of wonder that had become horror before she turned five years old. Sydni, who had been in the trade before her, and her mother before *her*; Sydni, who had borne her through the activities of one nameless father after another. And one of them had carried the genes that had produced the eyes. Forever eyes.

She tried desperately to get drunk, but it wouldn't happen. More bread, another bowl, another chigger and rum — and nothing happened. But she sat in the booth, determined not to go back into the alleys. The alien might be looking for her, might still demand its credits' worth of sex and awfulness, might try once again to force her to drink the drink it had called "mooshsquash." The chill that came over her made her shiver; brain movies with forever eyes were vivid and always fresh, always now, never memories, always happening *then.*

She cursed her mother and thought the night would probably never end.

An old woman, a very old woman, a woman older than anyone born on the day she had been born, nodded her head to her dressers. They began covering her terrible nakedness with expensive fabrics. She had blue hair. She did not speak to them.

Now that he had overcome the problems of pulse pressure on the association fibers of the posterior lobe of the brain, he was certain the transplanted mutations would be able to mould the unconscious cerebral image of the seen world into the conscious percept. He would make no guarantees for the ability of the recipient to cope with the flux of the external world in all its complexity — infinitely more complicated as "seen" through the mutated transplant eyes — but he knew that his customer would hardly be deterred by a lack of such guarantees. They were standing in line. Once he had said, "The unaided human eye under the best possible viewing conditions can distinguish ten million different color surfaces; with transplants the eye will perceive ten *billion* different color surfaces; or more," they were his. They . . . *she* . . . would pay anything. And anything was how much he would demand. Anything to get off this damned planet, away from the rot that was all expansion had left of Earth.

There was a freehold waiting for him on one of the ease-colonies of Kendo IV. He would take passage and arrive like a prince from a foreign land. He would spin out the remaining years of his life with pleasure and comfort and respect. He would no longer be a Knoxdoctor, forced to accept ghoulish assignments at inflated prices, and then compelled to turn over the credits to the police and the sterngangs that demanded "protection" credit.

He needed only one more. A fresh pair for that blue-haired old harridan. One more job, and then release from this incarceration of fear and desperation and filth. A pair of gray-blue eyes. Then freedom, in the ease-colony.

It was cold in Dr. Breame's Knox Shop. The tiny vats of nutrients demanded drastically lowered temperatures. Even in the insulated coverall he wore, Dr. Breame felt the cold.

But it was always warm on Kendo IV.

And there were no prongers like Grebbie and Berne on Kendo IV. No strange men and women and children with eyes that glowed. No still-warm bodies brought in off the alleys, to be hacked and butchered. No vats with cold flesh floating in nutrient. No filth, no disgrace, no payoffs, no fear.

He listened to the silence of the operating room.

It seemed to be filled with something other than mere absence of sound. Something deeper. A silence that held within its ordered confines a world of subtle murmurings.

He turned, staring at the storage vats in the ice cabinet. Through the nearly transparent film of frost on the see-through door he could discern the parts idly floating in their nutrients. The mouths, the filaments of nerve bundles, the hands still clutching for life. There were sounds coming from the vats.

He had heard them before.

All the voiceless voices of the dead.

The toothless mouths calling his name: *Breame, come here, Breame, step up to us, look at us, come nearer so we can talk to you, closer so we can touch you, show you the true cold that waits for you.*

He trembled . . . surely with the cold of the operating room. *Here, Breame, come here, we have things to tell you: the dreams you helped end, the wishes unanswered, the lives cut off like these hands. Let us touch you, Dr. Breame.*

He nibbled at his lower lip, willing the voices to silence. And they went quiet, stopped their senseless pleading. Senseless, because very soon Grebbie and Berne would come, and they would surely bring with them a man or a woman or a child with glowing blue-gray eyes, and then he would call the woman with blue hair, and she would come to his Knox Shop, and he would operate, and then take passage.

It was always warm, and certainly it would always be quiet. On Kendo IV.

Extract from the brief of the Plaintiff in the libel suit of 26 Krystabel Parsons vs. Liquid Magazine, Liquid Newsfax Publications, LNP Holding Group, and 311 unnamed Doe personages.

from *Liquid Magazine* (uncredited profile):

Her name is 26 Krystabel Parsons. She is twenty-sixth in the line of Directors of Minet. Her wealth is beyond measure, her holdings span three federations, her residences can be found on one hundred and fifty-eight worlds, her subjects numberless, her rule absolute. She is one of the last of the unchallenged tyrants known as power brokers.

In appearance she initially reminds one of a kindly old grandmother, laugh-wrinkles around the eyes, blue hair uncoiffed, wearing exo-braces to support her withered legs.

But one hour spent in the company of this woman, this magnetism, this dominance . . . this force of nature . . . and all mummery reveals itself as cheap disguise maintained for her own entertainment. All masks are discarded and the Director of Minet shows herself more nakedly than anyone might care to see her.

Ruthless, totally amoral, jaded beyond belief with every pleasure and distraction the galaxy can provide, 26 Krystabel Parsons intends to live the rest of her life (she is one hundred and ten years old, and the surgeons of O-Pollinoor, the medical planet she caused to have built and staffed, have

promised her at least another hundred and fifty, in exchange for endowments whose enormity staggers the powers of mere gossip) hell-bent on one purpose alone: the pursuit of more exotic distractions.

Liquid Magazine managed to infiltrate the entourage of the Director during her Grand Tour of the Filament recently (consult the handy table in the front of this issue for ready conversion to your planetary approximation). During the time our correspondent spent with the tour, incidents followed horn-on-horn in such profusion that this publication felt it impossible to enumerate them fully in just one issue. From Porte Recoil at one end of the Filament to Earth at the other — a final report not received as of this publication — our correspondent has amassed a wealth of authenticated incident and first-hand observations we will present in an eleven-part series, beginning with this issue.

As this issue is etched, the Director of Minet and her entourage have reached PIX and have managed to elude the entire newsfax media corps. *Liquid Magazine* is pleased to report that, barring unforeseen circumstances, this exclusive series and the final report from our correspondent detailing the mysterious reasons for the Director's first visit to Earth in sixty years will be the only coverage of this extraordinary personality to appear in fax since her ascension and the termination of her predecessor.

Because of the history of intervention and censorship attendant on all previous attempts to report the affairs of 26 Krystabel Parsons, security measures as extraordinary as the subject herself have been taken to insure no premature leaks of this material will occur.

Note Curiae: Investigation advises subsequent ten installments of series referred to passim foregoing extract failed to reach publication. Entered as Plaintiff Exhibit 1031.

They barely had time to slot their credits and follow her. She paid in the darkness between bursts of light from the globes overhead; and when they were able to sneak a look at her, she was already sliding quickly from the booth and rushing for the iris. It was as if she knew she was being pursued. But she could not have known.

"Berne . . ."

"I see her. Let's go."

"You think she knows we're onto her?"

Berne didn't bother to answer. He slotted credits for both of them, and started after her. Grebbie lost a moment in confusion and then followed his partner.

The alley was dark now, but great gouts of blood-red and sea-green light were being hurled into the passageway from a top-mixer joint at the corner. She turned right out of Poke Way and shoved through the jostling crowds lemming toward Yardey's Battle Circus. They reached the mouth of the alley in time to see her cut across between rickshas, and followed as rapidly as they could manage through the traffic. Under their feet they could feel the throbbing of the machinery that supplied power to WorldsEnd. The rasp of circuitry overloading mixed faintly with the clang and shrieks of Yardey's sonic come-ons.

She was moving swiftly now, off the main thoroughfare. In a moment Grebbie was panting, his stubby legs pumping like pistons, his almost-neckless body tilted far forward, as he tried to keep up with lean Berne. Chew Way opened on her left and she moved through a clutch of tourists from Horth, all painted with chevrons, and turned down the alley.

"Berne . . . wait up . . ."

The lean pronger didn't even look back. He shoved aside a barker with a net trying to snag him into a free house and disappeared into Chew Way. The barker caught Grebbie.

"Lady, please . . ." Grebbie pleaded, but the scintillae in the net had already begun flooding his bloodstream with the desire to bathe and frolic in the free house. The barker was pulling him toward the iris as Berne reappeared from the mouth of Chew Way and punched her in the throat. He pulled the net off Grebbie, who made idle, underwater movements in the direction of the free house. Berne slapped him. "If I didn't need you to help carry her . . ."

He dragged Grebbie into the alley.

Ahead of them, Verna stopped to catch her breath. In the semi-darkness her eyes glowed faintly; first gray, a delicate ash-gray of moth wings and the decay of Egypt; then blue, the fog-blue of mercury light through deep water and the lips of a cadaver. Now that she was out of the crowds, it was easier. For a moment, easier.

She had no idea where she was going. Eventually, when the special sight of those endless memories had overwhelmed her, when her eyes had become so well-adjusted to the flash-lit murkiness of the punchup pub that she was able to see . . .

She put that thought from her. Quickly. Reliving, that was almost the worst part of *seeing*. Almost.

. . . when her sight had grown that acute, she had fled the punchup, as she fled *any* place where she had to deal with people. Which was why she had chosen to become one of the few blousers in the business who would service aliens. As disgusting as it might be, it was infinitely easier with these malleable, moist creatures from far away than with men and women and children whom she could see as they . . .

She put that thought from her. Again. Quickly. But she knew it would return; it always returned; it was always there. The worst part of *seeing.*

Bless you, Mother Sydni. Bless you and keep you.

Wherever you are; burning in tandem with my father, whoever he was. It was one of the few hateful thoughts that sustained her.

She walked slowly. Ignoring the hushed and urgent appeals from the rag mounds that bulked in the darkness of the alley. Doorways that had been melted closed now held the refuse of WorldsEnd humanity that no longer had anything to sell. But they continued needing.

A hand came out of the black mouth of a sewer trap. Bone fingers touched her ankle; fingers locked around her ankle. "Please . . ." The voice was torn out by the roots, its last film of moisture evaporating, leaves withering and curling in on themselves like a crippled fist.

"Shut up! Get away from me!" Verna kicked out and missed the hand. She stumbled, trying to keep her balance, half turned, and came down on the wrist. There was a brittle snap and a soft moan as the broken member was dragged back into the darkness.

She stood there screaming at nothing, at the dying and useless thing in the sewer trap. "Let me alone! I'll kill you if you don't leave me alone!"

Berne looked up. "That her?"

Grebbie was himself again. "Might could be."

They started off at a trot, down Chew Way. They saw her faintly limned by the reflection of lights off the alley wall. She was stamping her foot and screaming.

"I think she's going to be trouble," Berne said.

"Crazy, you ask me," Grebbie muttered. "Let's cosh her and have done with it. The Doc is waiting. He might have other prongers out looking. We get there too late and we've wasted a lot of time we could of spent —"

"Shut up. She's making such a hell of a noise she might've already got the police on her."

"Yeah, but . . ."

Berne grabbed him by the tunic. "What if she's under bond to a sterngang, you idiot?"

Grebbie said no more.

They hung back against the wall, watching as the girl let her passion dissipate. Finally, in tears, she stumbled away down the alley. They followed, pausing only to stare into the shadows as they passed a sewer trap. A brittle, whispering moan came from the depths. Grebbie shivered.

Verna emerged into the blare of drug sonics from a line of top-mixers that sat horn-on-horn down the length of Courage Avenue. They had very little effect on her; drugs were in no way appealing; they only intensified her *seeing*, made her stomach hurt, and in no way blocked the visions. Eventually, she knew, she would have to return to her coop; to take another customer. But if the slug alien was waiting . . .

A foxmartin in sheath and poncho sidled up. He leaned in, bracing himself with shorter appendages against the metal sidewalk, and murmured something she did not understand. But the message was quite clear. She smiled, hardly caring whether a smile was considered friendly or hostile in the alien's mind. She said, very clearly, "Fifty credits." The foxmartin dipped a stunted appendage into the poncho's roo, and brought up a liquid shot of an Earthwoman and a foxmartin without its shield. Verna looked at the liquid and then away quickly. It wasn't likely the alien in the shot was the same one before her; this was probably an example of vulpine pornography; she shoved the liquid away from her face. The foxmartin slid it back into the roo. It murmured again, querulous.

"*One hundred* and fifty credits," Verna said, trying hard to look at the alien, but only managing to retain a living memory of appendages and soft brown female flesh.

The foxmartin's fetching member slid into the roo again, moved swiftly out of sight, and came up with the credits.

Grebbie and Berne watched from the dimly shadowed mouth of Chew Way. "I think they struck a deal," Grebbie said softly. "How the hell can she do it with something looks like that?"

Berne didn't answer. How could people do *any* of the disgusting things they did to stay alive? They *did* them, that was all. If anyone really had a choice, it would be a different matter. But the girl was just like him: she did what she had to do. Berne did not really like Grebbie. But Grebbie could be pushed and shoved, and that counted for more than a jubilant personality.

They followed close behind as the girl with the forever eyes took the credits from the alien and started off through the crowds of Courage Avenue. The foxmartin slid a sinuous coil around the girl's waist. She did not look at the alien, though Berne thought he saw her shudder; but even from that distance he couldn't be certain. Probably not: a woman who would service *things.*

Dr. Breame sat in the far corner of the operating room, watching the movement of invisible life in the Knox Shop. His eyes flicked back and forth, seeing the unseen things that tried to reach him. Things without all their parts. Things that moved in liquid and things that tried to crawl out of waste bins. He knew all the clichés of seeing love or hate or fear in eyes, and he knew that eyes could reflect none of those emotions without the subtle play of facial muscles, the other features of the face to lend expression. Even so, he *felt* his eyes were filled with fear. Silence, but movement, considerable movement, in the cold operating room.

The slug alien was waiting. It came up out of a belowstairs entranceway and moved so smoothly, so rapidly, that Berne and Grebbie froze in a doorway, instantly discarding their plan to knife the foxmartin and prong the girl and rush off with her. It flowed up out of the dark and filled the twisting passageway with the wet sounds of its fury. The foxmartin tried to get between Verna and the creature; and the slug rose up and fell on him. There was a long moment of terrible sucking sounds, solid matter being turned to pulp and the marrow being drawn out as bones caved in on themselves, filling the lumen with shards of splintered calcium.

When it flowed off the foxmartin, Verna screamed and dodged away from the mass of oily gray worm oozing toward her. Berne began to curse; Grebbie started forward.

"What the hell good can you do?" Berne said, grabbing his partner. "She's gone, dammit!"

Verna ran toward them, the slug alien expanding to fill the passageway, humping after her like a tidal wave. Yes, yes, she had *seen* that crushed, empty image . . . *seen* it a thousand times, like reflections of reflections, shadow auras behind the reality . . . but she hadn't known what it meant . . . hadn't *wanted* to know what it meant! Servicing aliens, as perverted and disgusting as it was, had been the only way to keep sane, keep living, keep a vestige of hope that there was a way out, a way off Earth. Yes, she had seen the death of the foxmartin, but it hadn't mattered . . . it wasn't a *person*, it was a creature, a thing that could not in sanity have sex with a human, that *had to have* sex with a human, in whatever twisted fashion it found erotic. But now even that avenue was closing behind her . . .

She ran toward them, the slug alien making its frenzied quagmire sounds of outrage and madness, rolling in an undulant comber behind her. Grebbie stepped into her path and the girl crashed into him, throwing them both against the wall of the passageway. Berne turned and ran back the way he had come. An enormous shadow, the slug alien, puffed up to three times its size, filled the foot of the passage.

Berne saw lights ahead, and pounded toward them.

Underfoot, he felt a rumbling, a jerking of parts and other parts. There was a whining in his ears, and he realized he had been hearing it for some time. Then the passageway heaved and he was hurled sidewise, smashing face-first into the melted window of a condemned building. He flailed wildly as the metal street under him bucked and warped, and then he fell, slamming into the wall and sliding down. He was sitting on the bucking metal, looking back toward the foot of the passage, when the slug alien suddenly began to glow with blue and orange light.

Verna was lying so close to the edge of the creature that the heat it gave off singed her leg. The fat little man she'd run into was somewhere under the alien. Gone now. Dead. Like the foxmartin.

But the slug was shrieking in pain, expanding and expanding, growing more monstrous, rising up almost to the level of second-storey windows. She had no idea what was happening . . . the whining was getting louder . . . she could smell the acrid scent of ozone, burning glass, boiling lubricant, sulfur . . .

The slug alien glowed blue, orange, seemed to be lit from inside, writhed hideously, expanded, gave one last, unbelievable sucking moan of pain and *burned.* Verna crawled away on hands and knees, down the egress passage, toward the light, toward the shape of a man just getting to his feet, looking dazed. Perhaps he could help her.

"The damned thing killed Grebbie. I didn't know what was happening. All at once everything was grinding and going crazy. The power under the streets had been making lousy sounds all night, I guess it was overloading, I don't know. Maybe that filthy thing caused it somehow, some part of it got down under the sidewalk plate and fouled the machinery, made it blow out. I think it was electrocuted . . . I don't know. But she's here, and she's got what you need, and I want the full amount; Grebbie's share and mine both!"

"Keep your voice down, you thug. My patient may arrive at any moment."

Verna lay on the operating table, watching them. *Seeing* them. Shadows behind shadows behind shadows. All the reflections. *Pay him, Doctor*, she thought, *it won't matter. He's going to die soon enough. So are you. And the way Grebbie bought it will look good by comparison. God bless and keep you, Sydni.* She could not turn it off now, nor damp it with bowl, nor hide the images in the stinking flesh of creatures from other worlds of other stars. And in minutes, at best mere moments, they would ease her burden; they would give her peace, although they didn't know it. *Pay him, Doctor, and let's get to it.*

"Did you have to maul her?"

"I didn't maul her, damn you! I hit her once, the way I hit all the others. She's not damaged. You only want the eyes anyhow. Pay me!"

The Knoxdoctor took credits from a pouch on his coverall and counted out an amount the pronger seemed to find satisfactory. "Then why is she so bloody?" He asked the question as an afterthought, like a surly child trying to win one final point after capitulating.

"Creep off, Doc," Berne said nastily, counting the credits. "She was crawling away from that worm. She fell down half a dozen times. I told you. If you're not satisfied with the kind of merchandise I bring you, get somebody else. Tell me how many other prongers could've found you a pair of them eyes in gray-blue, so quick after a call?"

Dr. Breame had no time to form an answer. The iris dilated and three huge Floridans stepped into the Knox Shop, moved quickly through the operating room, checked out the storage area, the consultation office, the power bins, and came back to stand near the iris, their weapons drawn.

Breame and Berne watched silently, the pronger awed despite himself at the efficiency and clearly obvious readiness of the men. They were heavy-gravity-planet aliens, and Berne had once seen a Floridan put his naked fist through a plasteel plate two inches thick. He didn't move.

One of the aliens stepped through the iris, said something to someone neither Berne nor the doctor could see, and then came back inside. A minute later they heard the sounds of a group moving down the passage to the Knox Shop.

26 Krystabel Parsons strode into the operating room and waved her guard back. All but the three already in the Knox Shop. She slapped her hands down to her hips, locking the exo-braces. She stood unwaveringly and looked around.

"Doctor," she said, greeting him perfunctorily. She looked at the pronger.

"Greetings, Director. I'm pleased to see you at long last. I think you'll find —"

"Shut up." Her eyes narrowed at Berne. "Does this man have to die?"

Berne started to speak, but Breame quickly, nervously answered. "Oh, no; no indeed not. This gentleman has been most helpful to our project. He was just leaving."

"I was just leaving."

The old woman motioned to one of the guards, and the Floridan took Berne by the upper arm. The pronger winced, though the guard apparently was only serving as butler. The alien propelled Berne toward the iris, and out. Neither returned.

Doctor Breame said, "Will these, uh, gentlemen be necessary, Director? We have rather delicate surgery to perform and they . . ."

"They can assist." Her voice was flat as iron.

She dropped her hands to her hips again, flicking up the locking levers of the exo-braces that formed a spiderweb scaffolding around her withered legs. She strode across the operating room toward the girl immobilized on the table, and Breame marveled at her lack of reaction to the cold in the room: he was still shivering in his insulated coverall, she wore an ensemble made of semi-transparent, iridescent flow bird scales. But she seemed oblivious to the temperature of the Knox Shop.

26 Krystabel Parsons came to Verna and looked down into her face. Verna closed her eyes. The Director could not have known the reason the girl could not look at her.

"I have an unbendable sense of probity, child. If you cooperate with me, I shall make certain you don't have a moment of regret."

Verna opened her eyes. The Director drew in her breath.

They were everything they'd been said to be.

Gray and blue, swirling, strange, utterly lovely.

"What do you see?" the Director asked.

"A tired old woman who doesn't know herself well enough to understand that all she wants to do is die."

The guards started forward. 26 Krystabel Parsons waved them back. "On the contrary," she said. "I not only desire life for myself . . . I desire it for you. I'm assuring you, if you help us, there is nothing you can ask that I will refuse."

Verna looked at her, *seeing* her, knowing she was lying. Forever eyes told the truth. What this predatory relic wanted was: everything; who she was willing to sacrifice to get it was: everyone; how much mercy and kindness Verna could expect from her was: infinitesimal. But if one could not expect mercy from one's own mother, how could one expect it from strangers?

"I don't believe you."

"Ask and you shall receive." She smiled. It was a terrible stricture. The memory of the smile, even an instant after it was gone, persisted in Verna's sight.

"I want full passage on a Long Driver."

"Where?"

"Anywhere I want to go."

The Director motioned to one of the guards. "Get her a million credits. No. Five million credits."

The guard left the Knox Shop.

"In a moment you will see I keep my word," said the Director. "I'm willing to pay for my pleasures."

"You're willing to pay for my pain, you mean."

The Director turned to Breame. "Will there be pain?"

"Very little, and what pain there is, will mostly be yours, I'm afraid." He stood with hands clasped together in front of him: a small child anxiously trying to avoid giving offense.

"Now, tell me what it's like," 26 Krystabel Parsons said, her face bright with expectation.

"The mutation hasn't bred true, Director. It's still a fairly rare recessive . . ." Breame stopped. She was glaring at him. She had been speaking to the girl.

Verna closed her eyes and began to speak. She told the old woman of *seeing*. Seeing directions, as blind fish in subterranean caverns see the change in flow of water, as bees see the wind currents, as wolves see the heat auras surrounding humans, as bats see the walls of caves in the dark. Seeing memories, everything that ever happened to her, the good and the bad, the beautiful and the grotesque, the memorable and the utterly forgettable, early memories and those of a moment before, all on instant recall, with absolute clarity and depth of field and detail, the whole of one's past, at command. Seeing colors, the sensuousness of airborne bacteria, the infinitely subtle shadings of rock and metal and natural wood, the tricksy shifts along a spectrum invisible to ordinary eyes of a candle flame, the colors of frost and rain and the moon and arteries pulsing just under the skin; the intimate overlapping colors of fingerprints left on a credit, so reminiscent of paintings by the old master, Jackson Pollock. Seeing colors that no human eyes have ever seen. Seeing shapes and relationships, the intricate calligraphy of all parts of the body moving in unison, the day melding into the night, the spaces and spaces between spaces that form a street, the invisible lines linking people. She spoke of *seeing*, of *all* the kinds of seeing except. The stroboscopic view of everyone. The shadows within shadows behind shadows that formed terrible, tortuous portraits she could not bear. She did not speak of that. And in the middle of her long recitation the Floridan guard came back and put five million credits in her tunic.

And when the girl was done, 26 Krystabel Parsons turned to the Knoxdoctor and said, "I want her kept alive, with as little damage as possible to her faculties. You will place a value on her comfort as high as mine. Is that clearly understood?"

Breame seemed uneasy. He wet his lips, moved closer to the Director (keeping an eye on the Floridans, who did not move closer to him). "May I speak to you in privacy?" he whispered.

"I have no secrets from this girl. She is about to give me a great gift. You may think of her as my daughter."

The doctor's jaw muscles tensed. This was, after all, ***his*** operating room! *He* was in charge here, no matter how much power this unscrupulous woman possessed. He stared at her for a moment, but her gaze did not waver. Then he went to the operating table where Verna lay immobilized by a holding circuit in the table itself, and he pulled down the anesthesia bubble over her head. A soft, eggshell-white fog instantly filled the bubble.

"I must tell you, Director, now that she cannot hear us —"

(But she could still *see*, and the patterns his words made in the air brought the message to her quite distinctly.)

"— that the traffic in mutant eyes is still illegal. Very illegal. In point of fact, it is equated with murder, and because of the shortage of transplantable parts the MediCom has kept it a high crime; one of the few for which the punishment is vegetable cortexing. If you permit this girl to live you run a terrible risk. Even a personage of *your* authority would find it most uncomfortable to have the threat of such a creature wandering loose."

The Director continued staring at him. Breame thought of the unblinking stares of lizards. When she blinked he thought of the membranous nictitating eyelids of lizards.

"Doctor, the girl is no problem. I want her alive only until I establish that there are no techniques for handling these eyes that she can help me to learn."

Breame seemed shocked.

"I do not care for the expression on your face, Doctor. You find my manner with this child duplicitous, yet you are directly responsible for her situation. You have taken her away from whomever and wherever she wished to be, you have stripped her naked, laid her out like a side of beef, you have immobilized her and anesthetized her; you plan to cut out her eyes, treat her to the wonders of blindness after she has spent a lifetime seeing far more than normal humans; and you have done all this not in the name of science, or humanity, or even curiosity. You have done it for credits. I find the expression on your face an affront, Doctor. I advise you to work diligently to erase it."

Breame had gone white, and in the cold room he was shivering again. He heard the voices of the parts calling. At the edges of his vision things moved.

"All I want you to assure me, Doctor Breame, is that you can perform this operation with perfection. I will not tolerate anything less. My guards have been so instructed."

"I'm perhaps the only surgeon who *can* perform this operation and guarantee you that you will encounter no physically deleterious effects. Handling the eyes *after* the operation is something over which I have no control."

"And results will be immediate?"

"As I promised. With the techniques I've perfected, transfer can be effected virtually without discomfort."

"And should something go wrong . . . you can replace the eyes a second time?"

Breame hesitated. "With difficulty. You aren't a young woman; the risks would be considerable; but it *could* be done. Again, probably by no other surgeon. And it would be extremely expensive. It would entail another pair of healthy eyes."

26 Krystabel Parsons smiled her terrible smile. "Do I perceive you feel underpaid, Doctor Breame?"

He did not answer. No answer was required.

Verna saw it all, and understood it all. And had she been able to smile, she would have smiled; much more warmly than the Director. If she died, as she was certain she would, that was peace and release. If not, well . . .

Nothing was worse than life.

They were moving around the room now. Another table was unshipped from a wall cubicle and formed. The doctor undressed 26 Krystabel Parsons and one of the two remaining Floridans lifted her like a tree branch and laid her on the table.

The last thing Verna saw was the faintly glowing, vibrating blade of the shining e-scalpel, descending toward her face. The finger of God, and she blessed it as her final thoughts were of her mother.

26 Krystabel Parsons, undisputed owner of worlds and industries and entire races of living creatures, jaded observer

of a universe that no longer held even a faint view of interest or originality, opened her eyes.

The first things she saw were the operating room, the Floridan guards standing at the foot of the table staring at her intensely, the Knoxdoctor dressing the girl who stood beside her own table, the smears of black where the girl's eyes had been.

There was a commotion in the passageway outside. One of the guards turned toward the iris, still open.

And in that moment all sense of *seeing* flooded in on the Director of Minet. Light, shade, smoke, shadow, glow, transparency, opacity, color, tint, hue, prismatics, sweet, delicate, subtle, harsh, vivid, bright, intense, serene, crystalline, kaleidoscopic, all and everything at once!

Something else. Something more. Something the girl had not mentioned, had not hinted at, had not wanted her to know! The shadows within shadows.

She *saw* the Floridan guards. *Saw* them for the first time. Saw the state of their existence at the moment of their death. It was as if a multiple image, a strobe portrait of each of them lived before her. The corporeal reality in the front, and behind — like endless auras radiating out from them but superimposed over them — the thousand images of their futures. And the sight of them when they were dead, how they died. Not the action of the event, but the result. The hideous result of having life ripped from them. Rotting, corrupt, ugly beyond belief, and all the more ugly than imagination because it was *seen* with forever eyes that captured all the invisible-to-normal-eyes subtleties of containers intended to contain life, having been emptied of that life. She turned her head, unable to speak or scream or howl like a dog as she wished, and she *saw* the girl, and she *saw* the doctor.

It was a sight impossible to contain.

She jerked herself upright, the pain in her withered legs barely noticeable. And she opened her mouth and forced herself to scream as the commotion in the passageway grew louder, and something dragged itself through the iris.

She screamed with all the unleashed horror of a creature unable to bear itself, and the guards turned back to look at her with fear and wonder . . . as Berne dragged himself into the room. She *saw* him, and it was worse than all the rest, because it was happening *now*, he was dying *now*, the vessel was emptying *now*! Her scream became the howl of a dog. He could not speak, because he had no part left in his face that could make a formed sound come out. He could see only imperfectly; there was only one eye. If he had an expression, it was lost under the blood and crushed, hanging flesh that formed his face. The huge Floridan guard had not been malevolent, merely Floridan, and they were a race only lately up from barbarism. But he had taken a long time.

Breame's hands froze on the sealstrip of the girl's tunic and he looked around her, saw the pulped mass that pulled itself along the floor, leaving a trail of dark stain and viscous matter, and his eyes widened.

The Floridans raised their weapons almost simultaneously, but the thing on the floor gripped the weapon it had somehow — amazingly, unpredictably, impossibly — taken away from its assassin, and it fired. The head of the nearest Floridan caved in on itself, and the body jerked sidewise, slamming into the other guard. Both of them hit the operating table on which the Director of Minet sat screaming, howling, savaging the air with mortal anguish. The table overturned, flinging the crippled old woman with the forever eyes to the floor.

Breame knew what had happened. Berne had not been sent away. It had been blindness for him to think she would leave *any* of them alive. He moved swiftly, as the remaining Floridan struggled to free himself of the corpse that pinned him to the floor. The Knoxdoctor had the e-scalpel in his hand in an instant, palmed it on, and threw himself atop the guard. The struggle took a moment, as Breame sliced away at the skull. There was a muffled sound of the guard's weapon, and Breame staggered to his feet, reeled backward, and crashed into a power bin. Its storage door fell open and Breame took two steps into the center of the room, clutching his chest. His hands went inside his body; he stared down at the ruin; then he fell forward.

There was a soft bubbling sound from the dying thing that had been the pronger, Berne, and then silence in the charnel house.

Silence, despite the continued howling of 26 Krystabel Parsons. The sounds she made were so overwhelming, so gigantic, so inhuman, that they became like the ticking of a clock in a silent room, the thrum of power in a sleeping city. Unheard.

Verna heard it all, but had no idea what had happened. She dropped to her knees, and crawled toward what she thought was the iris. She touched something wet and pulpy with the fingertips of her left hand. She kept crawling. She touched something still-warm but unmoving with the fingertips of her right hand, and felt along the thing till she came to hands imbedded in soft, rubbery ruin. To her right she could faintly hear the sound of something humming, and she knew the sound: an e-scalpel, still slicing, even when it could do no more damage.

Then she had crawled to an opening, and she felt with her hands and it seemed to be a bin, a large bin, with its door open. She crawled inside and curled up, and pulled the door closed behind her, and lay there quietly.

And not much later there was the sound of movement in the operating room as others — who had been detained for reasons Verna would never know — came and lifted 26 Krystabel Parsons, and carried her away, still howling like a dog, howling more intensely as she saw each new person, knowing eventually she would see the thing she feared seeing the most. The reflection of herself as she would be in the moment of her dying; and knowing she would still be sane enough to understand and appreciate it.

From extreme long shot, establishing; trucking in to medium shot, it looks like this:

Viewed through the tracking devices of PIX's port authority clearance security system, the Long Drive vessel sits in its pit, then slowly begins to rise out of its berth. White mist, or possibly steam, or possibly ionized fog billows out of the pit as the vessel leaves. The great ship rises toward the sky as we move in steadily on it. We continue forward, angle tilting up to hold the Long Driver in medium shot, then a fast zoom in on the glowing hide of the ship, and dissolve through to a medium shot, establishing the interior.

Everyone is comfortable. Everyone is watching the planet Earth drop away like a stained glass window through a trapdoor. The fisheye-lens of the stateroom iris shows Worlds-End and PIX and the polar emptiness and the mottled ball of the decaying Earth as they whirl away into the darkness.

Everyone sees. They see the ship around them, they see one another, they see the pages of the books they read, and they see the visions of their hopes for good things at the end of this voyage. They all see.

Moving in on one passenger, we see she is blind. She sits with her body formally erect, her hands at her sides. She wears her clothing well, and apart from the dark smudges that show beneath the edge of the stylish opaque band covering her eyes, she is a remarkably attractive woman. Into tight closeup. And we see that much of her grace and attractiveness comes from the sense of overwhelming peace and containment her features convey.

Hold the closeup as we study her face, and marvel at how relaxed she seems. We must pity her, because we know that blindness, not being able to see, is a terrible curse. And we decide she must be a remarkable woman to have reconciled such a tragic state with continued existence.

We think that if we were denied sight, we would certainly commit suicide. As the darkness of the universe surrounds the vessel bound for other places.

"If the doors of perception were cleansed everything would appear to man as it is, infinite."
William Blake, "The Marriage of Heaven and Hell," 1790

As our knowledge of the universe grows, we find not only new wonders but also unsuspected terrors. Recently a book on "black holes" was published, explaining the awesome discoveries that have been made in recent years about these collapsed stars whose mass is so enormous that it prevents even light from escaping their gravity-wells. The question that was asked first in the book was, "Will they destroy the entire universe by sucking in every atom of matter in existence?"

Well, the answer is no: the mass of black holes isn't *that* great. But if a spaceship were to venture near a black hole, the danger of being drawn into it would be very real indeed . . . and Brian Aldiss has imagined the eerie result of such a cosmic accident.

Brian W. Aldiss is one of the premiere talents of modern science fiction, the author of such novels as *The Long Afternoon of Earth*, *Greybeard*, and *Frankenstein Unbound*, as well as the critically acclaimed history of science fiction, *Billion-Year Spree*.

The Dark Soul of the Night

Brian W. Aldiss

As CORDRON CONTINUED across the plain, he became aware of a line in the ground, scrawled like a snake across old paving. He continued to walk. He ignored the boom-boom-boom, boom-boom-boom in his head.

He kept heading due south as always, checking direction occasionally by the compass on the arm of his suit. After another kilometer, the line in the ground was still beside him. Now it was drawn more boldly.

Cordron did not look back. His ears gave him all the data he needed regarding the disposition of his family. Over the months, he had trained himself not to look back, except at long measured intervals, even when the quarrels of the children were at their most shrill.

At present, his two older boys were staying fairly close behind him. The rest of the family spread back over perhaps half a kilometer, with Katti in the middle by the sledge, interfering in the quarrels and generally managing to exacerbate them. Behind her straggled the younger members of the family, with the exception of the wandering girl of the party, who was keeping up with the biggest boys for a while, and the sick member, who rode on the sledge. It had become a convention of the Journey that one child should be sick each day and ride on the underpowered sledge.

Their voices came clearly to Cordron. He took no notice of what they were saying, merely using the sounds as gauges for morale and possible trouble. He could effectively still arguments by slowing or hastening his own pace, depending on the time of day to decide which would be more immediately effective. So long had they been on the move that the family responded automatically to his pacesetting, even in the heat of a quarrel.

He heard a piping dispute on whether hopping animals could be taught to walk. He heard a continuation of the endless saga of the imaginary Eegey Bumptoe, who had set out to swim around the galaxy, after first flooding it with H_2O provided by a sentient hosepipe nebula. He heard the low conversation concerning the difficulty of getting to know — *really* getting to know — other people in starflight. He heard the older boys speculating on what the natives of this planet would do and look like if there *were* any natives. All this Cordron heard and did not listen to. He kept walking toward the south. Sooner or later, they must reach the equatorial guardian posts. Such posts had been soft-landed on every deserted planet.

As the hours passed, the talk became more intermittent, the family more strung out. The line in the ground widened into a crack. It widened only gradually, sometimes changing direction or sending out tributary cracks that crossed the group's path.

There was nothing to be seen ahead except the dull mist, which closed in at two hundred paces in all directions. Cordron generally kept his gaze on the mist, still watchful after all these months. Just in case something came charging out of the mist at them, or there was a sudden change in the nature of the terrain. Morn or night, he never forgot the heavy responsibility he carried.

The continual boom-boom-boom, boom-boom-boom was still audible in the background. They had heard it as soon as they crawled out of the wrecked ship; it had been so continuously with them that they heard it now only with conscious effort. Like the laboring of blood in their inner ears, the boom-boom-boom, boom-boom-boom was part of them.

At first they had believed the noise to be the sound of immense but distant machinery. There was something about the planet — so large yet so lacking in mass, so distant from the inhabited galaxy, so near annihilation — that made it seem unlikely and therefore artificial. The machine-sound might have been coming from some cavernous, alien-forged interior.

During the early weeks of the Journey, the boom-boom-boom, boom-boom-boom had slowly increased in volume. The mist had been thicker then. As it intensified, the sound increased; mist and sound had grown to become the presence of the planet. Some titanic thing ahead labored at its existence, not caring who knew of it. Their sleep was shot through with dreadful speculations as to what shape it took.

Katti had come to him and begged that they might proceed in a different direction. He had refused. In their perilous situation, logic must be sole arbiter. Their only hope lay to the south. They could not waste their lives in desolation; if there was anything of intelligence controlling the machinery — if it was machinery they could hear — then they must try to establish rapport with it; their salvation lay no other way. So he had said, assembling them together. They went ahead on unaltered compass reading. That night, she crept close to him, weeping in his arms for fear. All the while, the boom-boom-boom, boom-boom-boom continued unaltered, unchanging in its tedious rhythm. The nights were the worst: at night, when the mists blew away, they saw both the Phantom and that terrible thing that ruled over all their troubles.

Days later, they were walking in their normal formation when the ground became broken and sloped downward into mist. Cordron called a halt and went forward with one of the boys. They came to a place where the ground tumbled away into an abyss. Its depths were filled with mist, swirling restlessly in updrafts. The rest of the party gathered cautiously on the lip of the land, staring uneasily down.

Finally, the mists parted for a time. Not far below their

feet lay a foamless cavern-dark ocean, its uncapped waves moving in steady progression toward the shore. Every wave was the same size as the one before, as the one after, as the one after that. Each came in briskly, yet without haste, as if it had crossed many thousands of miles of open and unpunctuated sea — as it undoubtedly had — to cast itself into formlessness again as it delivered its particular boom to the perpetual boom-boom-boom, boom-boom-boom.

The family stood for a long while staring at that fish-free vat of planetary waters. Even Cordron could not pull himself away.

"It's the primordial ocean," one of the younger boys said. He repeated the phrase at intervals. Uncertain whether he had the correct word, he occasionally varied the phrase, remarking instead, "It's the primordinal ocean."

The time came when they turned away. The compass was reset on a new bearing and Cordron got them all into action again with the aid of Alouette. Since then, they had moved parallel to the coast, hoping for a way due south. The incessant mist and the incessant boom-boom-boom, boom-boom-boom accompanied them.

Where the mist parted ahead, Cordron saw that the crack in the ground widened sharply. He stopped and inspected the increased division, over which he could still tread with a full pace. The rocky ground, which appeared parched despite the prevailing mists, showed sheer sides where it parted; as yet, the gap was only a meter deep.

He summoned Alouette and told her to round up the party. They straggled toward him, waiting indifferently on either side of the crack. None of them showed curiosity, he noted, although one of the smaller girls climbed down into the crack with little shrieks, perching on its edge and calling to another sister to join her.

"The crack is getting wider by the kilometer," Cordron said. "There's no danger, but you must all stay on this side of it. Otherwise you will eventually become cut off from the rest of the family and have to make a long detour. So stay on this side of the crack. Okay? On we go again."

And off they want. As the party again began to string out, he heard their comments without looking back. As usual, they resented the mildest guidance. Everyone grumbled about him. He bore them no resentment. He was leader of the party, a natural target for their anxieties, and their dislike of him helped to unite them. He walked steadily on, noting when the widening crack forced them to deviate slightly from southwest. He wondered if the mist was dispersing, but the unhurried boom-boom-boom, boom-boom-boom continued unfalteringly as ever. He told himself that he would endure as the noise endured; sometimes he became confused in his thoughts and believed the noise to be the regular impulse of starflier engines.

The older boys were close behind him once more. He estimated them to be some hundred meters behind. His oldest son said, "He's mad, he's parablasting mad. Poor old *shoat* believes he's still walking across that deadly planet."

He heard one of the others saying, "Too much responsibility — broke his mind. Just broke his mind. Doesn't know where he is. . . ."

They had said it before, he recalled. Cordron risked a

glance back over his shoulder, trying not to meet their gaze. Then he looked ahead again, bewildered. The boys appeared very close, almost leaning over him in some impossible manner; yet they were also far away.

Rannaroth, he thought; Rannaroth bears a curse with it.

The boys were losing their grip on reality. He did not allow himself to wonder if he could deliver them before everyone lost his sanity. The Journey must occupy his whole mind. Just concentrate on getting to the equator; ignore the boys — and Rannaroth.

Nevertheless, the concept of the planet they traversed oppressed him. Cordron was an agriculturist, specializing in protein mutagenesis, and he knew very little about the universe across which he and his family were being shipped. What he had managed to learn had been gleaned from lifeboat readouts as the little ship plunged from its doomed mother and hurtled down to crash-land, its electronics burned out in the stratosphere. Planet X was large and largely nonmetallic, with a small eccentric iron core. It pursued a narrow elliptic orbit about its sun, Wexo, in a year as long as ten Earth-years.

Planet X had just passed perihelion. Now it was slowing and heading away from Wexo. The long winter was setting in, a winter that would mean the death of every living thing. Spring would not come again for another six or so Earth-years. The family had signaled their position as they fled from the starflier; but space was vast. They were far from civlization and civilization's outposts; if rescue did not come soon, the family would die. The thought of that long slow winter, of death by starlight, came very close to Cordron's mind, so he kept his party on the move for almost as long as Wexo burned in the shrouded skies.

Night came stealthily. Just as the seasons moved sluggishly from one phase to the next, so did the day, expiring in wreaths of brown, gray, and purple. They pitched camp on the endless plain, erecting the inflatable tents stashed away on the sledge. Katti supervised the heating of the evening meal. When the meal was eaten, one of the boys read from a poem — the telecoders were useless — after which all the family joined in a sing-along.

As they settled down for sleep, the usual night wind rose, whining about the tents as it drove the mist away. Cordron stood for a while, arms wrapped around his chest, watching the night clear; the sense of claustrophobia that assailed him in daylight hours eased a little.

He was about to turn in when Katti joined him, slipping an arm about his waist. Cordron was impatient, he hardly knew why. Ever since the Journey began, she seemed incongruous, almost irrelevant. Just as the Journey brought out his qualities, he could not help feeling that it obliterated hers.

"How long have we been on the move?" she asked, in a tone meant to ingratiate. Annoyed by the question, he answered her gruffly.

"What happens when we've walked right around the planet once?" she continued. "Do we start again?"

"Don't be silly, dear. There will be automatic posts at the equator."

They stood in silence. He thought with regret that she must feel as isolated as he, yet he could do nothing about it.

He loved her; he could do nothing about that either, until they had escaped from Planet X.

"I dread the nights," she said. "Rannaroth will be visible soon. And the — the Phantom. . . ."

Every evening, she told him she dreaded the nights. Most evenings, they stood together and watched for the Phantom; it was their only contact throughout the day.

When they slept, the Phantom hung over them, heavy, lowering, a dead weight on their spirits, as if the night had a dark soul. While the wind rose and the persistent afterglow, debris from ancient worlds, fluttered overhead, Cordron felt again the oppression he never shook off. He had trained himself not to voice his thoughts to any of the family.

They straggled back over the plain, through the mist, and involuntarily he uttered a groan.

"It's all right, David," she said. "It's all over, the Journey's over. We're safe, they picked us up, we reached the guardian post." She mopped his forehead. Wexo was a pallid disk like a sick-bay emergency light.

He struggled to grasp what she was saying. All he could hear was that machinelike noise, boom-boom-boom, boom-boom-boom.

He shook his head. "It's getting you down, Katti. The boys are the same. Never fear — we'll see it through. I'll see you through. The Journey isn't endless."

He could hardly make out her face. It was distorted, as if affected by the endless boom-boom-boom, boom-boom-boom.

Pushing her away, he stared up at the sky. The afterglow was clearing as the planetary penumbra washed across it.

There in the sky the terrible darkness of Rannaroth was revealed, boring its great circle out of the stars.

Here on the edge of the galaxy, he was looking back into the pearly heart of it. The outline of the black hole was easily visible. It seemed to pulsate slightly, to wear a halo — an atmospheric effect, he thought, every night uncertain whether or not he was correct. Every night, that terrible gravitational well dominated the sky of Planet X, ascending toward zenith as the planet forged toward its autumn solstice. Every night, it dominated his wakeful sleep, permeated his dreams. It was comparatively close, so that in his nightmares he saw Wexo slipping into it.

From Rannaroth they had escaped, if it counted as escape. The starflier's trajectory toward a new world had been miscalculated by a few seconds of arc, and it had been drawn into that maw. The lifeboats had blasted free just in time to escape annihilation, as the mother ship sank below the event horizon.

For the family in the lifeboat, existence beckoned. For the starflier, life and time had ceased, both wiped off the slate of possibility. Other lifeboats, too, had been drawn into the trap.

Cordron stared up at the black hole in the stars, wrestling with vaguely formed relativisitic ideas in his head. Up *there*, in some bizarre way, the starflier's crew were definitively dead to the outside world — yet within their own skulls they would still be falling inward toward Rannaroth's nucleus for years. But years, like space and sanity, were meaningless terms beyond the event horizons of the hole.

True night came. Up *there*, it was perpetual night. And

now Cordron could make out the image of the starflier. The ship itself had been sucked into the hole. Its image remained, isolated at the frozen point where light became stationary. The image hung there like a hollow fly in an old spiderweb.

He shook his head to see it clearly. There it was, the Phantom, the ghost of a brilliant ship with some five thousand passengers and crew, dead months ago! Every night, the Phantom grew as the hole grew, occupying all his mind.

In the morning, they took the usual instrumental scan for metallic objects ahead of them on the planetary surface. Every morning, nothing. The guardian posts established somewhere on the equator were still beyond range of their detectors. They loaded all the equipment onto the sledge and started off again.

It was a matter of walking beside the crack. The fissure was all of a half-kilometer wide and almost as deep, as far as could be discerned through the mists. They went on southwest, the weary column extending as the morning progressed and Wexo rose higher.

"I'll get you there if we go on forever," Cordron said.

He heard his wife say something and did not turn his head. She was many meters behind him, lagging with the wandering child, he knew, yet it was as if she spoke in his ear.

"It's all right," she said. "The Journey's over, David. We're almost home. We're safe!"

He kept on, ignoring their voices, eyes staring ahead, jaw set.

Humanity has undergone remarkably few physical changes in the five thousand years since the dawn of recorded history: our average height has grown a few inches as a result of dietary improvements and our average life expectancy has been extended by greater medical knowledge, but that's about all. Yet the science of genetics is still in its infancy, and it seems probable that future centuries will find scientists manipulating the chromosomes that determine our physical makeup. What might happen if such experiments get out of hand?

George R. R. Martin has leapt into science fiction prominence in recent years with such stories as *A Song for Lya*, for which he won the Hugo Award in 1975. He continues to get better, too, as this dark adventure in Earth's far future shows.

In the House of the Worm

George R. R. Martin

FOR AGES PAST remembering the House of the Worm had been lost in decay, and that was as it should be, for decay is but one name of the White Worm himself. So the *yaga-la-hai*, the worm-children, only smiled and went on as always, though the tapestries rotted on the walls of their endless burrows and their numbers dwindled each year, though meat grew ever more scarce, and the very stone around them turned to dust. In the high burrows with slit windows, awash with the red dimness of the vast dying ember above, they came and went and lived their lives. They tended their torches and held their masques, and made the sign of the worm whenever they passed near the dark windowless burrows where the grouns were said to mutter and lie in wait (for the halls and tunnels of the House of the Worm were reputed to be infinite, descending as far below the earth as the black sky ascends above, and the *yaga-la-hai* claimed only a few of its many ancient chambers).

It was taught to the worm-children that the White Worm comes for all in the end, but he crawls most slowly and in the long decay there is fine feasting and the bright sickly colors of rot. Such wisdom was enforced by the current Manworm and his bronze knights, even as their ancestors had enforced it for generations untold. Thus did the House of the Worm endure, though the grouns might crawl below and the sun burn out above.

Every fourth year the brightest and wittiest and highest-born among the *yaga-la-hai* would gather in the Chamber of Obsidian to view the sun and feast in its dying rays. The chamber was the only place for such a brilliant masque. It was high in the House of the Worm, so that all the tunnels leading to it slanted upward, and the floor and ceiling and three of the walls were sheets of fused obsidian, cold and shiny as a mirror and dark as death. For the four-years-less-a-day that passed between the Sun Masques, the lesser-born worm-children, called torch-tenders, worked tirelessly in the chamber, polishing and rubbing, so that when the bronze knights came to fire the torches their reflections would gleam in the black glass around them. Then the guests would assemble, a thousand strong in gay costumes and fantastic masks, and the obsidian would bend and distort their bright faces and graceful forms, until they were a whirling motley of demons dancing in a great black bottle.

And that was only part of the Chamber of Obsidian. There was more; there was the window. It occupied all of the fourth wall behind the sand-filled hollow where the Manworm coiled; crystal clear the window was, yet stronger than any glass they knew. Nowhere in the House of the Worm was there another window a fraction of its size. The glass, if glass it was, looked out on a dead and desolate plain where no wind stirred; all darkness there, all empty, though there were crumbling stone shapes near the sometimes-seen horizon that might or might not be ruins. It was hard to tell; the light was very bad.

The sun filled half the sky; from one end of the horizon to the other it arched, bulking high enough to touch the zenith. Above it was unending black sky, broken by a handful of stars. The sun itself was a softer black, the color of ash, except in the few places where it still lived. Rivers ran across it, twisting ribbons of glowing red, veins of fire across its tired face. The worm-children had studied them once, in the long-ago years when they played with telescopes, and each of the burning channels had once had a name, though most had been forgotten. Where the rivers met and joined, sometimes smoldering orange lakes could be seen, and there were other places where gleams of red and yellow pulsed beneath the ash-dark crust. Best of all were the seas, two huge oceans of angry red that grew smaller and darker with every masque; one up near the rim continued on the side never seen, and a second burned near the sun's waist and often outlined the maybe-ruins on the horizon.

From noon, when the Sun Masque commenced (all times were arbitrary with the worm-children, for the light was the same, day and night), until midnight, all the feasters would be masked, even the Manworm, and long curtains of heavy red velvet would be drawn across the great window, to hide the sun. Silent torch-tenders would bring out the feast on black iron trays, and arrange it on the long table: heavy mushrooms in cream sauce, subtly flavored puffballs, tiny slugs wrapped in bacon, fragrant green wine alive with struggling spiceworms, fried crawlers, roast hole-hogs from the Manworm's royal larder, hot mushroom bread, a thousand other delicacies. And, as a centerpiece, if they were lucky, a plump six-limbed groun-child (or two!), just below the age of puberty, basted with care and served whole, its meat white and juicy. The guests would eat until they could eat no more, joke and laugh through their veils and dominoes, then dance beneath the torches for hours on end while obsidian ghosts mocked their movements in the walls and floor. When finally midnight came, the unmasking began. And when all had bared their faces, the bronze knights would carry the reigning Manworm to the fourth wall, and he would pull the curtain cord (if he still had hands—if not, the knights would pull it) and unmask the sun.

The Manworm that year was the Second Vermentor, fourteenth of his line to rule the *yaga-la-hai* from the High Burrow in the House of the Worm. He had reigned a dozen years already, and soon his time would be at an end, for the priest-surgeons had done their holy work all that while, and there was nothing left to purify but the too-human head that lolled atop the sinuous writhing torso. Soon he would be one with the White Worm. But his son was ready.

The bronze knight Groff, huge and stiff in armor, carried Vermentor to the window and acted as his hands. The velvet slid back smoothly, and the old sun was revealed as the Manworm intoned the ancient worship words and the worm-children gathered round to look.

Annelyn, surrounded by his friends and acolytes, was one of the closest to the glass, as was fitting. Annelyn was always to the front. He was a slim and glorious youth, tall and graceful. All the highborn *yaga-la-hai* had soft mocha skins, but Annelyn's was the softest of them all. Most of his fellows had blond or red-blond hair, but Annelyn's was the brightest yellow-gold; it crowned his head in delicate sculptured ringlets. Many worm-children had blue eyes, but none so blue and deep as Annelyn's.

He was the first to speak after the curtains were drawn. "The black parts grow," he observed to those around him, in a light, clear voice. "Soon our curtains will not be needed. The sun now masks itself." He laughed.

"It dies," said Vermyllar, a gaunt boy with hollow cheeks and flaxen hair who worried far too much. "My grandfather told me once that there was a time when the black plains were smoky red and the seas and rivers were white fire, painful to look upon." Vermyllar's grandfather had been second son of the Manworm, and thus knew all sorts of things that he passed on to his grandson.

"Perhaps it was so," Annelyn said, "but not in his time, I

would wager, or even that of *his* grandfather." Annelyn had no blood ties with the line of the Manworm, no secret sources of knowledge, but he was always quite sure of his opinions, and his friends — Vermyllar and stout Riess and beautiful Caralee — thought him the wisest and wittiest of men. Once he had killed a groun.

"Don't you worry about the sun dying?" Caralee asked him, tossing blond curls easily as she turned to face him. She looked enough like Annelyn to be his sister-twin; perhaps that was why he wanted her so. "About the burrows growing cold?"

Annelyn laughed again, and Riess laughed with him. (Riess *always* laughed with Annelyn, though Annelyn suspected that the fat boy seldom understood the joke.) "The sun was dying long before I came into the House of the Worm, and it will continue dying long after I have left," he said, turning away from the window. He was splendid that night, in his costume of pale blue silk and spidergray with the crest of theta stitched above his breast.

"As for the cold," Annelyn continued, as he led his three companions back toward the feasting table, "I don't believe that the old sun has anything to do with heat, one way or the other."

"It does," said Vermyllar, who had come in brown rags like a mushroom farmer. He and Caralee matched Annelyn stride for stride across the obsidian, their images hurrying at their feet. Riess puffed along behind, struggling to keep up in the mock armor of a bronze knight.

"Did your grandfather tell you that?" Annelyn asked. Riess laughed.

"No," Vermyllar said, frowning. "But notice, Annelyn, how the sun resembles a hot coal stolen from a firebox?"

"Perhaps," Annelyn said. He paused beside the winebowl and filled two cut-crystal goblets with the rich green wine, fishing in the bowl until he found two worms tied in a writhing knot. He scooped them into Caralee's drink, and she smiled at the proposition when he handed her the glass. The second goblet, with a single worm, he sipped himself as he turned back to Vermyllar.

"If the sun is nothing but a large coal," Annelyn continued, "then we need not worry, since we have plenty of smaller coals on hand, and the torch-tenders can always fetch up more from the dark."

Riess giggled. He had set his knight's helm on the table and was now munching from a platter of spiced spiders.

"That may be true," Vermyllar said. "But then you admit the sun is a coal, that it helps to warm the burrows."

"No," said Annelyn. "I merely conjectured. In fact, I think the sun is an ornament of sorts, set in the sky by the White Worm to provide us with light and an occasion for masques."

Suddenly, startlingly, there was laughter, coarse and low. Annelyn's smile turned abruptly to a frown when he realized that whoever it was laughed not at his wit, but at *him*. He drew himself up and turned in annoyance.

When he saw who laughed, however, he only raised a glass (and a fine blond eyebrow) in mock salute.

The Meatbringer (so they called him—if he had a truer name, he did not use it) ceased his laughter; there was a silence. He was a low, broad man, a head shorter than Annelyn and uglier than any of the *yaga-la-hai*, with his straight white hair, mottled pink-brown skin, and enormous flat nose. His orange and crimson image etched by torchlight in the obsidian was taller and more handsome than the Meatbringer himself had ever been.

He had come to the Sun Masque alone and out of costume, horribly out of place, admitted only because of the groun-child he had provided. Instead of masque finery, he wore his familiar suit of milk-white leather, sewn from the skin of dead grouns, with a colorless half-cloak of woven grounhair. Throughout the House of the Worm his boast was known: that he dressed in the skin and hair of grouns he had himself slain. He was the Meatbringer, who went alone into deep burrows without windows.

Caralee looked at him very curiously. "Why did you laugh?" she asked.

"Because your friend is funny," the Meatbringer said. His voice was too low, too coarse. Annelyn felt a trifle absurd, being insulted by a mottled man who grumbled in the manner of a torch-tender. And now a curious knot of people began to gather around them; the *yaga-la-hai* were always interested in the odd, and the Meatbringer was oddest of all. Besides, everyone had grown tired of viewing the sun.

"I'm always pleased to find someone who appreciates wit," Annelyn said, studiously attempting to turn the Meatbringer's veiled insult into a compliment.

"I do appreciate wit," the Meatbringer said. "I wish I could find some. This masque is witless."

He had no subtlety, Annelyn decided. "Only in comparison," he said. "You are perhaps accustomed to delightful banter with the grouns?"

Riess giggled, and the Meatbringer smiled savagely at him. "The grouns have more wit than your simpering friend, and more knowledge than you."

There was stifled laughter around them, whether at the absurdity of the Meatbringer's words or at the insult, Annelyn could not be sure. "You know groun secrets, then?" he said lightly.

"They have them, yes. And I know them, yes. And more."

"The grouns are animals," Vermyllar put in.

"As are you," said the Meatbringer.

Vermyllar flushed. "I wear rags tonight, but only for the masque. My grandfather was a son of the Manworm."

"Better your grandfather than you," the Meatbringer said.

This time Caralee laughed. Annelyn looked at her, horrified that she could find humor in such coarseness. "You mock the honor?" he said. "The great knowledge? The responsibilities?"

"*I* have heavier responsibilities," the Meatbringer said in a level voice. "As do the others who try to go down and bring back groun meat. The Manworm has only musty ritual duties that no one understands. As to his great knowledge, I have more of *that* too. The *yaga-la-hai* know nothing of themselves or of the House of the Worm except half-truths and distorted lies. And *honor*?" He gestured toward the window. Groff, in his intricately wrought rust-dark armor, still stood stiffly with the Manworm in his arms. Another of the bronze knights was closing the curtains; the dancing had resumed.

"Yes?" Annelyn prompted, blankly.

"The honor is all hideous pain," the Meatbringer said, and as if to emphasize his statement the Manworm suddenly lifted his head and his white body began to thrash wildly in Groff's arms. "Under the knives again and again, each time waking as less of a man. And it ends in deformity and death. Honor?"

Now the crowd around them looked shocked, except for a handful who had listened to the Meatbringer before and knew his amusing irreverence. "The Manworm is purified," Riess said. (Try as he might, he was dull and orthodox underneath, and they all knew it.) "He is becoming one with the White Worm!"

Annelyn shushed him; he thought of himself as inclined to the cynical and the shocking. "Perhaps you have a point about the honor," he said to the Meatbringer. "Freethinkers like myself have also questioned the custom, but . . ."

Again the Meatbringer began to laugh at him, throwing his head back and roaring. Annelyn flushed darkly and drained his wine with a snap — worm and all — as he fought to stay calm.

"*Freethinker*!" the Meatbringer finally choked out when his laughter had subsided. "I doubt that you have ever had a free thought. You are nothing, less than the Manworm." He pushed past Annelyn and began to fill his own goblet with wine.

"I have killed a groun," Annelyn said, quickly, not thinking, regretting the words the instant they were spoken.

The Meatbringer simply turned on him, and grinned, and then *everyone* began to laugh. There was no need to comment; all of the worm-children knew that the Meatbringer had killed perhaps a hundred grouns, not one. Even Caralee joined the general laughter, though Vermyllar and Riess were mercifully silent. Tall as he was, Annelyn suddenly felt as if the Meatbringer towered over him. He glanced down and saw his own face looking up, foolish and shaken, from the cold obsidian.

The Meatbringer studied Caralee with approval. "Share my bed tonight," he said suddenly, as blunt as any torch-tender. Annelyn looked up again, shocked. The Meatbringer had no shame. Caralee wore blue-and-spidergray, even as he did; clearly they were together. And he had given her the cup of the mating-worms!

She looked at Annelyn briefly, then seemingly dismissed him with a toss of her bright curls, turning toward the Meatbringer. "Yes," she said, strange excitement in her voice. Then they went off together onto the vast black mirror of the dance floor to whirl and writhe and slide together in the intricate ancient patterns of the *yaga-la-hai.*

"He has humiliated us," Annelyn said furiously to Riess and Vermyllar as he watched the Meatbringer clumsily parody Caralee's graceful moves.

"We should go to the Manworm," Vermyllar suggested.

Riess said nothing, but his round face was screwed up in agitation as he reached for another spiced spider.

"No," Annelyn said. Beyond the sea of wriggling dancers in all their gorgeous colors, Groff had returned the Manworm to his sand pit. Squat torch-tenders were moving around the fringes of the chamber, snuffing two flames of every three. Soon the obsidian grew clouded by darkness, and the bright reflections faded to red streaks on the glass.

In shadowed corners, a few bold couples had already commenced the unmasking-of-the-bodies; others soon would follow their example. Annelyn had planned to unmask Caralee. Now he was alone.

"Why not?" Vermyllar was demanding. "You heard him. He called me an animal, and I am the grandson of a man who might have been Manworm."

Annelyn waved him quiet. "You will have your revenge," he said. "But my way, *my* way." His deep blue eyes stared across the chamber. The Meatbringer was leading Caralee off toward a corner. "My way," he repeated. Then: "Come." And he led them from the room.

They met the next morning, early, amid the dust and fading tapestries of the seldom-used Undertunnel, which connected most of the main burrows of the *yaga-la-hai* before curving away on its long descent into infinity. Annelyn was the first to arrive. He was dressed all in shiny-smooth black, with a hood of the same color to hide his bright hair. His only concession to vanity was a gold theta, embroidered on his breast. A belt of black rope held both rapier and stiletto.

Riess soon materialized, in a tight-fitting shirt of mail and leather and a heavy cloak of spidergray. He and Annelyn sat together on a stone floor across from a black mouth that belched hot, moist air at them through a rusty grid. Light, such as there was, came from scattered torches set in bronze hands on the walls, and from the windows — narrow slits in the ceiling, twenty feet above their heads — that leaked a dim red radiance. The windows were set ten feet apart all along the Undertunnel, until where it began to sink. Once, as a boy, Annelyn had piled junk high in the middle of a burrow and climbed to look out, but there had been nothing to see — the glass, even as the stone of the walls, was thicker than a man is tall. It was fortunate that *any* light got through.

Vermyllar was late. Annelyn sat cross-legged, his eyes on the hanging tapestries whose images had all turned to mottled gray. Riess was very excited. He was talking about imaginative tortures they could inflict on the Meatbringer. "When we catch him, we should hang him upside down by running cords through his ankles," the stout youth suggested. "Then we can buy a pot of bloodworms from the surgeon-priests and set them all over his body to drink him dry."

Annelyn let him prattle, and finally Vermyllar appeared, wearing black and gray and carrying a torch and a long dagger. The other two sprang up to greet him.

"I should not have come," Vermyllar said. His face was very drawn, but he seemed to relax a bit in the presence of his friends. "I am the great-grandson of the Manworm himself," he continued, sheathing his dagger while Riess took the torch from him, "and I should not listen to you, Annelyn. We will all be eaten by grouns."

"The Meatbringer is not eaten by grouns, and he is only one while we are three together," Annelyn said. He started down the Undertunnel, toward the endless gray where the bands of red light no longer striped the stone, and the others followed.

"Are you sure he comes this way?" Vermyllar asked. They passed another of the square black mouths, and their cloaks stirred and flapped in its warm breath. Vermyllar gestured at the opening. "Perhaps he climbs down one of those, to where the grouns live."

"They are very sheer and very hot," Annelyn told him, "and he would fall or burn if he went that way. Besides, many people have seen the Meatbringer come and go along the Undertunnel. I asked among the torch-tenders."

They passed beneath the last window; ahead, the Undertunnel slanted down and the ceiling was featureless. Vermyllar stopped in the last zone of light.

"Grouns," he said. "Annelyn, there are *grouns* down there. Away from the windows." He licked his lips.

"I have killed a groun," Annelyn reminded him. "Besides, we have talked of this. We have our torch, and each of us is carrying matches. There are old torches all along the tunnel, so many can be lit. Besides, the grouns never come this high. No one has seen a groun in the Undertunnel for a lifetime."

"People vanish every month," Vermyllar insisted. "Mushroom farmers. Groun hunters. Children."

Annelyn began to sound cross. "Groun hunters go deep, so of course they are caught. The others, well, who knows? Are you afraid of the dark?" He stamped a boot impatiently.

"No," said Vermyllar, and he came forward to join them again. But he rested his hand on his dagger hilt.

Annelyn did not start again immediately. He walked over to the curving wall, and reached up, pulling a torch from a bronze hand. He lit it from the flames of the torch Riess was carrying, and suddenly the light was doubled. "There," he said, handing the torch to Vermyllar. "Come."

So they began to walk down the long dark burrow as it curved and sank, almost imperceptibly: past tapestries that hung in rotten threads and others that were thick tangles of matted fungus; past an endless series of torch-clutching hands (every other one empty, and only one in fifty alight); past countless bricked-up tunnel mouths and a few whose bricks had shattered or turned to dust; past the invisible warmth of the air ducts one after another. They walked in silence, knowing that their voices would echo, hoping that the dust beneath would muffle the sounds of their footsteps. They walked until they had lost sight of the last window, and for an hour after that. And finally they reached the spot where the Undertunnel came to an end. Ahead were two square doorways whose metal doors had long since crumbled into flakes of rust. Riess thrust a torch through one and saw only a few heavy cables, twisting around in tangles and sinking into the yawning darkness of a shaft that fell down and down. Startled, he pulled back and almost dropped the torch.

"Careful," Annelyn warned.

"What is it?" Riess said.

"Perhaps a trap," Vermyllar suggested. He thrust his own torch into the second doorway, and they saw a stone stair that descended rapidy. "See? There were two doors here, once. An enemy or a groun might choose the wrong one, and fall down that shaft to its death. It was probably just an air shaft that they put a door on."

Annelyn moved over next to Riess. "No," he said, peering into the shaft. "There are ropes. And this shaft is cold." He shook his head, and his hood fell back, revealing blond curls that shone softly in the dancing torchlight. "No matter," he said. "We will wait here. Deeper than this and we *would* meet grouns. Besides, I do not know where that stair leads. So better to wait, and let the Meatbringer lead us."

"What?" Vermyllar was shocked. "You do not mean to take him here?"

Annelyn smiled. "Ha! That would be a child's revenge. No, we will follow him, deep into the country of the grouns. We will learn all his secrets, all the knowledge that he boasts of. We will see why he comes back and back again, always with meat, while other groun hunters vanish. *Then* we will kill him."

"You didn't say *that*," Riess objected, openmouthed.

"We've already come too far from the windows," Vermyllar said, and started to go on.

Annelyn laughed lightly. "Child," he said to Riess. "*I* came this far when I was half your age. This was where I killed my groun." He pointed to the stairway. "He came out of there, scrabbling on four of his legs, not the least afraid of my fire, and I met him with only my torch."

Vermyllar and Riess were both looking at the dark portal of the stairway. "Oh," said Riess.

"Really?" said another voice, from behind. Vermyllar dropped his torch, and pulled out his dagger. All three of them whirled.

On the edge of the light, a huge, red-bearded man dressed in black stood staring at them, a bronze ax on his shoulder. Without his armor, Annelyn hardly recognized him, but suddenly the memory came.

"Groff," he said.

The bronze knight nodded. "I have followed you all down the Undertunnel. You are very noisy."

They said nothing. Vermyllar picked up his fallen torch.

"So you mean to kill the Meatbringer?" Groff said.

"Yes," Annelyn said. "Do not interfere, Groff. I know the Meatbringer provides much grounmeat for the *yaga-la-hai,* but we shall do that too when we learn his secrets. The Manworm has no cause to take his side." His mouth was set stubbornly.

Groff chuckled, deep in his throat, and hefted his heavy ax. "Don't fret, little worm-child. You shall have your carrion. I too was sent to kill the Meatbringer."

"What?" Riess said.

"Did the Manworm order it?" Vermyllar asked eagerly.

"The Manworm thinks of nothing but his coming unity with the White Worm," Groff said. He smiled. "And of pain, perhaps. Perhaps he thinks of that. No, his advisers ordered it. The Meatbringer has too many mysteries about him. He is not truly of the *yaga-la-hai,* the advisers think, and he is not tranquil. He is ugly and disturbs things, and he lies. Moreover, since we first grew aware of the Meatbringer, two years ago, fewer and fewer groun hunters have returned from below, save him alone. Well, *I* have hunted grouns, once. I may not have been as deep as the Meatbringer, who says he has descended to where the bronze knights warred against the grouns a million years ago. I have not been that far, but I have run the groun-runs, and I am not frightened of dark burrows." He looked at Annelyn. "Did you truly meet a groun here?"

Annelyn felt the steady gaze of Groff's eyes, beneath their thick red brows. "Yes," he said, a little too quickly, afraid that somehow Groff knew the truth. The groun had been lying at the top of the stairs, mumbling its death rattle, when Annelyn had found it. The boy had watched, terrified, while the creature's six gangling limbs trembled fitfully (and briefly) and the moist sunken pools of flesh that the grouns had instead of eyes roamed back and forth, without purpose. When the carcass had been quite still, Annelyn had charred it with his torch, then dragged it back to the burrows of the *yaga-la-hai*.

Groff shook his head. "They seldom come past the groun-wall," the bronze knight said. "During the last years of my hunting, they seldom came at all. The Meatbringer must truly go deep." He smiled. "But so shall we."

"We?" It was Vermyllar.

Groff nodded. "I am not averse to help, and Annelyn's idea is a good one. We will learn the Meatbringer's secrets before we kill him." He waved his ax in a broad gesture. "Down the stair."

The doorway loomed pitch-black and ominous, and Annelyn began to feel nervous. It was one thing to impress Riess and Vermyllar with his bold plan to descend to groun country, but no doubt in time they would have talked him out of it. Perhaps the three of them would have fallen upon the Meatbringer *here* — beyond the light, true, but only a short way, and Annelyn had been here before. But to actually go *down* . . .

It was Vermyllar who protested. "No," he said, "I'm not going any deeper than this." He looked at Annelyn. "You kill the Meatbringer, or Groff can kill him, or Riess if he can, but he'll be just as dead without me along as with me. I'm going back."

"Down the stair," Groff said sternly. "I'll have no desertions."

Vermyllar stood fast. "My grandfather is a son of the Manworm," he said. "I do as I please." To Annelyn and Riess he made the sign of the worm, then with his torch in hand he started back the way they had come.

Groff made no move to stop him. "Down the stair," he repeated after Vermyllar's light had vanished behind a curve of the wall. They hurried to obey.

Down. The worst of all possible directions. Down. Where the grouns lay. Down. Away from light. Yet they went, and Annelyn remembered that even at the best of times, he disliked stairs. He was lucky, at that. Riess, holding the torch, had to go first.

At the foot of the stair was a narrow landing with two bricked-in doors, another gaping entrance to the still, cold shaft, and another stair. Down. There was another stair beyond that. Down. And another beyond *that.*

Finally they emerged. "Put out the torch," Groff said. Riess complied.

They stood clustered on one end of a slender metal bridge that spanned a cavernous chamber a hundred times the size of the Chamber of Obsidian. Far, far above was a vast roof of glass panes (each of them the size of the one behind the Manworm's pit, Annelyn thought) set in a latticework of black metal. The sun loomed over it, with its oceans of fire and plains of ash, so they did not need the torch.

There were other bridges, Annelyn saw — five of them; slim threads that swung from one black wall to the other, above a pool of some sluggish liquid that stirred and made noises just below their feet. And there was a sixth, or had been, but now it was shattered, and the twisted ribbon of its span hung down into the moving blackness below them.

There was a smell. Strong, thick, and sickly sweet.

"Where are we?" Riess whispered.

"The Chamber of the Last Light," Groff said brusquely. "Or so it is called in the lore of the bronze knights. But groun hunters call it the grounwall. This is the last and deepest place where the old sun can peer in. The White Worm created it to keep the grouns from the burrows of his children, some say."

Annelyn walked to the rail of the bridge. "Interesting," he said casually. "Are there no other ways for the grouns to climb up, then?"

"No more," Groff told him. "Once. But bronze knights sealed them with bricks and blood. Or so it is said." He pointed his ax toward the shadows on the far side of the bridge. "Across."

The span was narrow, barely wide enough for two men to walk abreast. Annelyn stepped forward hesitantly, reaching out to the guardrail for support. It came away in his hand, a small piece of metal tubing, eaten through by rust. He looked at it, stepped backward, then chucked it away, off into the liquid.

"The damp," Groff said, unconcerned. "The bridge itself has rust holes, so be careful where you step." His voice was stern and inflexible.

So Annelyn found himself edging forward again, step by careful step, out above the sloshing blackness into the abyss of dim red light. The bridge creaked and moved beneath his feet, and more than once he felt something give as he set down a tentative foot, so he was forced to pull back quickly and step somewhere else. Riess came after him, holding the useless rail tightly whenever there was a rail to hold. Groff cheerfully walked on the places the others had tested.

Halfway across, the bridge began to sway—slowly at first, then with greater speed. Annelyn froze, clutched for the rail, and looked over his shoulder at Groff.

The bronze knight swore. "Three is too much," he said. "*Hurry!*"

Not daring to run, Annelyn began to walk as quickly as he could, and as he did so the swaying got worse. He walked even faster, and behind him he could hear the others. At one point, there was a sudden snapping and a crunch, followed by a screech of pain. *Then* he ran, all but jumping the last few feet to the stone semicircle that anchored the bridge on the far side of the chamber. Only then, safe, did he turn back. Riess had hit a rust spot; his right leg had plunged right through the metal. Groff was helping him out. "Hold it steady," the bronze knight shouted, and Annelyn went back to the stone precipice and steadied the shaking bridge as best he could.

Soon Groff joined him, supporting a limping Riess. The leather he wore had saved him from serious injury, but the jagged metal edges had still cut into his leg, and there was some blood.

While Groff tended to him, Annelyn looked about. The

stone platform on which they stood was ringed by dark shapes, great square boxes that stood along its edge like a row of rotten teeth. He went to one. It was metal, scarred by rust and disuse, and studded by a dozen tiny glass windows, behind which was nothing but dust. There were holes in the boxes, too, and several of them had been smashed. Annelyn could make no sense of it.

Riess was on his feet again, looking shaken. "I dropped the torch," he said.

"There are others to be had," Groff said. "We could not have used ours, in any event. The Meatbringer would see its light. No, we must enter the groun-runs in the dark, and wait there until we see the light of *his* torch. Then we will follow that."

"What?" said Annelyn. "But Groff, that is madness. There will be grouns in the dark, perhaps."

"Perhaps," Groff replied. "Not likely, not this close to light, to the grounwall. Groun hunters, in my time and even before, had to go deeper to find prey. The upper runs are empty. But we will not go far." He pointed toward the wide black door that waited for them where the platform met the wall.

Annelyn drew his stiletto and went swiftly forward, not to look a coward. If a groun lurked in the blackness, he would be ready for it.

But there was nothing. Faintly, in the small light that still bled from the chamber, he saw the outline of three burrows, each darker than the one before.

"The left leads down," Groff said, "into the richer parts of the runs. The center is bricked-off and abandoned. We will wait there. We can watch the bridge, hidden by darkness, and follow the Meatbringer's torch when he passes."

He herded them forward, and they sat on the dusty stone to wait. The door to the Chamber of the Last Light faced them, like a dim red window; all else was black and silent. Groff sat unmoving, his ax across his lap and his legs crossed under him. Riess fidgeted. Annelyn put his back to the wall, so no grouns could creep up behind him, and toyed with his stiletto.

It was not long before he began to hear noises, soft mutters and low sounds, like the ugly voices of grouns grouping to attack them. But the tunnel was a solid blindness, and the harder he listened, the more the noise became blurred and indistinct. Footfalls? Or only Groff's breathing? Or perhaps it was the sound of the stirring liquid, not far off? Annelyn gripped his blade tighter. "Groff," he warned, but the other only silenced him.

He was remembering stories — of how the grouns could see in total darkness, of how they padded up so quietly on soft white feet and wrapped their six long limbs around straying *yaga-la-hai* — when the *other* noise began. Soft first, then louder; this could be no mistake. It was thin and ragged; it rose and fell, full of chokes and sobs. Groff heard it, too. Suddenly, silently, he was on his feet. Annelyn leaped up beside him, then Riess.

The bridge swayed slowly in the red window before them. Someone was coming.

The noise grew, and became more human. A voice, a real voice, warped by fear. Then Annelyn heard words: ". . . *please . . . not into the dark again . . . grouns . . . they'll . . .*

can't do . . ." And then, very clearly, "My grandfather was a son of the Manworm."

They saw. Vermyllar was coming across the bridge. Behind him, holding a long knife half-seen in the light, was the Meatbringer, squat and ugly in his suit of grounskin. "Quiet!" the Meatbringer said, and Vermyllar stumbled onto the safety of the stone, looking up fearfully at the black door that gaped before him.

Suddenly Annelyn felt Groff's hand on his chest, pushing, pushing. "Back," the knight whispered, oh-so-softly, and this time Annelyn gladly went deeper into the shadows. Something was wrong. Something was very, very wrong.

Neither Vermyllar nor the Meatbringer was carrying a torch.

"Get up," the Meatbringer said. "Get up and walk. I'm not going to carry you."

Vermyllar rose unsteady and whimpering. "Don't," he said. "It's *dark*. I can't *see*. Don't."

The Meatbringer pricked him with the knife. "In and to the left," he said. "Feel if you can't see, animal. *Feel.*" And Vermyllar went into the tunnel, groping for the wall, sobbing, seeming to look straight at Annelyn before he turned to the left. But the Meatbringer never glanced their way as he went by, prodding Vermyllar forward with his blade.

To Annelyn it seemed a solid hour that he stood in the black of the middle tunnel, but it could only have been minutes. Finally the sound of Vermyllar's protests and wails dwindled to a small noise down below them. Then Groff spoke. "No torch," he said, and even *his* stern voice seemed shaken. "The man's eyes are possessed by a groun."

"Are we going back?" Riess said.

"Back?" Groff was outlined in the red light of the door. "No. No. But *we* must see. A torch, we must have a torch. We will catch them. We know the way he went, and the Man-worm's great-grandson was making much lament."

"Why does he want Vermyllar?" Annelyn said, in a whisper. His wits had fled him.

"I can conjecture," Groff said. "But we will see." He gave orders, and the three of them began to roam the small length of burrow, feeling for torch grips. Riess found nothing but an air duct, but Annelyn's hands finally closed over a familiar bronze fist. It held a torch.

While Riess lit it, Annelyn turned to Groff. "A fist, the work of the *yaga-la-hai*, here, in the groun-runs. How is that, Groff?"

"These were not always groun-runs. The worm-children carved these burrows, a million years ago. The grouns drove them upward in a great war, or so it is said. The burrows that have always been the grouns' are different. Now the grouns cluster below, and the *yaga-la-hai* above; both were created many and strong, and both we and they have decayed, as all things great and small decay in the sight of the White Worm. So these tunnels and the Chambers of the Last Light and our Undertunnel are all empty where once they were full."

Riess, holding the torch, made the sign of the worm.

"Come," Groff said. "The burrow goes straight a long way, down and down, but it finally breaks, and we must not lose them."

So they began to walk — Riess with the torch and Groff

with his ax, Annelyn clutching his stiletto — and they made good speed. The burrow was utterly empty: a long, wide stretch of hot-mouthed air ducts and broken bronze fists that clutched at air. Twice they passed bones, whether groun or human Annelyn could not tell; the rest was all dark nothingness. Finally, when they reached a juncture where many tunnels met and branched, they could hear Vermyllar's weeping again, and they knew which way to choose.

They followed for a long time, losing the sound twice in the maze of interconnecting burrows, but each time quickly retracing their steps when the sobs began to grow faint. These, Annelyn realized with a shiver, were the groun-runs, the real things, and *he* was in them, descending to infinity. His blue eyes grew wide and sharp, and he watched everything in the flickering torchlight: the black beckoning squares of the tunnels they passed, the endless corroded fists, row on row, the carpets of dust that lay thick in some places and were strangely absent in others. Noises, too, he heard, as he had when they waited for the Meatbringer; soft mutters and softer footsteps, growls, the stirring of impossible cold winds in tunnels not chosen, and a dim, distant rumble like nothing he had ever imagined. Real noises, phantoms, fevers of a nervous brain — Annelyn did not know. He only knew that he heard them, so that the empty burrows seemed to fill with dark and unseen life.

There was no talk. They went down and around until Annelyn had lost track of their turnings. They descended twisted stone stairways, climbed down rusted ladders in echoing empty wells (always afraid that the rungs would snap), passed wide, slanted ramps and vast galleries that swallowed the light of their torch and furnished chambers where all the furniture was covered with dust and worm-rich rot. Once they walked through a high-ceilinged room much like a mushroom farm; but here the water-runs were dry and empty, and the long, sunken growing tanks held only a foul-smelling fungus that glowed a faint and evil green. Another hall they found was rich with tapestries, but each of the hangings was a gray rag that came apart at the touch.

The noises went ahead of them. Always.

Groff spoke only once, when they had stopped at the end of a bricked-in tunnel and were preparing to descend another of the round, black wells. "There are no grouns left," he muttered, more to himself than to them. "These are the places they once swarmed, and now they are empty." He shook his head, and his face was troubled. "The Meatbringer goes deep."

Neither Annelyn nor Riess replied. They found the rungs, and began to climb down. Then there were more tunnels.

Finally, though, they seemed to lose the way. At first the noise was ahead of them — Vermyllar's sobs, holding steady — but suddenly the sound grew less. Groff muttered something, and the three of them walked back to the last turning and chose another burrow. But they had gone only a few steps into the blackness when they lost the sound altogether. Back again they went, and into a third path; it proved silent and bricked-in.

"This was the right way," Groff insisted when they returned yet again to the junction, "the way we went first, though the noise *did* dwindle." He led them back, and they heard Vermyllar again, but once again the sound began to fade after they had followed it a short way.

Groff turned and paced down the tunnel. "Come," he said, and Riess hurried to his side with the torch. The knight was standing next to an air duct, its breath warm around them. The torch flame danced. Annelyn saw that the duct had no gridding. Then Groff reached inside. "A rope," he whispered.

Suddenly Annelyn realized that the sounds were coming from the shaft.

Groff fixed his ax to his belt, gripped the rope with both huge hands, and swung into the plunging dark. "Follow," he ordered; then, hand under hand, he vanished below. Riess looked at Annelyn, his eyes frightened, questioning.

"Spidersilk, no doubt," Annelyn said. "It will be strong. Put out the torch and come after." Then he, too, took the jerking rope.

The shaft was warm, but not as warm as Annelyn had imagined; he did not burn. It was also narrower than he had thought; when he grew tired, he could brace his knees against one side and his back against the other, resting for a moment. The rope had a life of its own, with Groff climbing below him and Riess above, but it was strong and new and easy to hold on to.

Finally, his feet kicked free; another level had been reached, and another grid was gone. Groff grabbed him and helped him out, and both of them helped struggling, panting Riess.

They were in a small junction, where three tunnels met at the huge metal doors of a great chamber. But Annelyn saw in a glance that the rope was the only way here; all three burrows were bricked-in. It was easy to see; the chamber doors were open, and light streamed out.

They watched from the shadows near the air duct, Groff crouching low with his ax in hand, Annelyn drawing his rapier.

The chamber was a large one, perhaps the size of the Chamber of Obsidian; there all resemblance ended. Inside, the Meatbringer had mounted a throne, firing two torches that slanted from brackets atop the backrest. Their flickering light mingled with a stranger radiance, a glowering purplish gleam that came from huge fungus-encrusted globes along the walls. Vermyllar was visible, sobbing incoherently, manacled to a wheeled bed close to the Meatbringer. From time to time his body shook as he strained fitfully against the shackles that held him down, but his captor ignored his struggles.

The rest of the chamber, in the curious mixed light, was like nothing Annelyn had ever encountered before. The walls were metal, time-eaten, rust-eaten, yet still bright in places. Panels of glass studded the high, dark flanks; a million tiny windows — most of them broken — winked at the flames. Along the side walls, fat transparent bubbles swelled obscenely near the ceiling. Some of these were covered by dripping, glowing growth, others were dry and broken, still others seemed full of some faintly moving fluid. A gulf of shadows and chaos lay between the walls. There were a dozen wheeled beds like the one Vermyllar was bound to, four huge pillars that rose to the ceiling amid a web of metal ropes and bars, a heavy tank of the sort the *yaga-la-hai* used for breeding foodworms, piles of clothing (some piles fresh, others covered by mold) and weapons and stranger things, metal cases with vacant glass eyes. In the center was the Meatbringer's throne, a high seat of green-black stone. A theta of some impossibly bright silver metal was sunk into the backrest, just above his head.

The Meatbringer had closed his eyes, and was leaning back on his throne. Resting, perhaps, Annelyn thought. Vermyllar still made noises; whimpers and groans and choking sounds, words that made no sense.

"He is mad," Annelyn whispered to Groff, certain that Vermyllar's noise would cover their speech. "Or he soon will be."

"Yes," Riess said, crawling close to them. "When are we going to save him?"

Groff turned his head to face Riess. "We are not," the bronze knight said, in a flat low voice. "He deserted us. He has no claim to my protection. It is better for the *yaga-la-hai* to watch and to follow, to see what the Meatbringer does with the great-grandson of a Manworm." His tone gave no room for appeal or argument.

Annelyn shivered, and moved away from Groff, who was once again watching intently with no flicker of movement. Briefly Annelyn had lost himself, allowed himself to trust and obey the older man, simply because Groff was a knight, because Groff knew the groun-runs. Suddenly he remembered his pride and his revenge.

Riess came to him. "*Annelyn,*" he said, his voice trembling. "What can we do?"

"Vermyllar brought this on himself," Annelyn whispered.

"But we shall rescue him, if we can." He had no idea how—it was one thing for Groff to face the Meatbringer with his great ax, but if the knight would not help . . .

Groff looked over his shoulder at them. He smiled.

Annelyn saw with a start that inside, the Meatbringer had risen. He was undressing, stripping off his suit of milk-white grounskin and his cloak of colorless grounhair. He turned his broad back to them, a well-muscled expanse of mottled flesh, while he tossed his clothing over an arm of his throne and rummaged through a pile of other clothes.

"Groff," Annelyn said firmly, "we must save Vermyllar, useless though he is. He amuses me. There are two of us, you know, and only one of you, and you need our help." Riess, behind him, was making faint choking noises.

Groff looked at them again, and sighed. "Do either of you know the way back up?" he asked, simply.

Annelyn fell silent. He did not know the way back, he realized. They would be lost in darkness. "Riess," he started to whisper.

The Meatbringer pulled on new clothing, and turned again, toward Vermyllar. A knife was in his hand. He looked different. He wore a suit of fine mocha leather, and over his shoulders was draped a long cape of curling hair that glinted softly like spun gold in the firelight. He muttered something, deep in his throat, with a voice such as the grouns used in all the tales that Annelyn had ever heard.

Vermyllar was suddenly shockingly sane. "No," he shouted. "No! My grandfather was a son of the Manworm!"

The Meatbringer slit his throat, and stepped nimbly aside as the blood came out in spurts and the body twitched. He caught some of the blood in a cup, and drank it with obvious satisfaction. The rest darkened the bed and ran across the floor, one trickle coming toward the worm-children as if it knew where they lurked in the shadow.

When Vermyllar was quite still, the Meatbringer loosed his shackles, and hoisted the body up on one broad shoulder. Annelyn watched, frozen in shock, and it came to him suddenly how often the Meatbringer had walked among the *yaga-la-hai*, carrying a groun carcass in just that way.

Groff glanced quickly around when the Meatbringer started toward them. None of the burrows offered even the promise of concealment. "Down the rope," the knight whispered urgently.

"*Down?*" Riess asked.

"No," said Groff. "Too late. He would find us still climbing, and cut the rope." He shrugged and straightened and hefted his ax. "No matter. We know all we need. He is not of the *yaga-la-hai*, as those close to the Manworm suspected. He brings meat to both men and grouns, this Meatbringer."

Annelyn stood at Groff's side, rapier in hand, balancing nervously on the balls of his feet. Riess, trembling, yanked free a knife. The Meatbringer appeared in the doorway, Vermyllar's corpse slung over his shoulder.

The three worm-children were cloaked by shadows, in the darkest part of the junction, while the Meatbringer had just come from a well-lit chamber. It was no advantage. He looked straight at them.

"So," he said, and he shrugged, letting Vermyllar's body slide to the floor with a thunk. His own blade, long and just recently wiped clean of blood, materialized in his hand.

"So," he said again. "Do the *yaga-la-hai* now come this deep?"

"Some," said Groff, lifting his ax lightly. Annelyn felt strangely light-headed and confident; bloodlust coursed through him. He would have his revenge, and Vermyllar's too. The Meatbringer could never stand before Groff. He was so squat and ugly, while the bronze knight was a near-giant, invulnerable even without his armor. Besides, *he* was there, and Riess too, though Riess hardly counted.

"What do you want?" the Meatbringer said, in the coarse low voice Annelyn remembered so well from the masque.

"To quiet your torch-tending tongue," Annelyn blurted, before Groff could answer. The Meatbringer looked at him for the first time, and chuckled.

"Who are you bringing meat to now?" Groff asked.

The Meatbringer chuckled again. "The grouns, of course."

"Are you a man? Or a new kind of groun?"

"Both. Neither. I have walked black tunnels alone for a long time. I was born a torch-tender, yes. But a special kind. Like the grouns, I see in total darkness. Like the *yaga-la-hai*, I can live and see in light. Both sorts of meat are pleasing." He showed a row of yellowed teeth. "I am flexible."

"One other question, before I kill you," Groff said. "The Manworm would know why."

The Meatbringer laughed; his thick body shook and the cape of golden ringlets danced on his shoulders. "The Manworm! *You* want to know, Groff, not your mindless master. *Why?* Because among the *yaga-la-hai* I am something less than a man, because among grouns I am something less than a groun. I am the first of the Third People. The *yaga-la-*

hai decline, as do the grouns, but I go among both and plant my seed" — he looked at Annelyn — "in those like Caralee, and in the groun-women. Soon there will be others like me. That is *why*. And to know. I know more than your Manworm, or you, more than the Great Groun. You live lies, but I have seen and heard all who live in the House of the Worm, and I believe none of it. The White Worm is a lie, do you know that? And the Manworm. I think I even know how that came to be. A pleasant tale. Shall I tell you?"

"The Manworm is the living flesh of the White Worm," Riess said in a shrill, almost hysterical voice. "The priests shape him in that image, purifying, making him more fit to lead."

"And less fit to live," the Meatbringer said. "Until the pain drives him mad or the surgery kills him. You, Groff? Do you believe that? Or you, freethinker? See. I *do* recall you."

Annelyn flushed and brandished his rapier. Groff was a fierce bearded statue of bronze-made-flesh. "So it is in the lore of the bronze knights," he said, "and we remember things the Manworm has forgotten."

"It shocks me that the Manworm remembers anything," the Meatbringer said. "But I have talked to knights, too, learned their 'secret' lore, listened to stories of a long-ago war. The grouns remember better. They have legends of the coming of the *yaga-la-hai*, who changed all the high burrows. The grouns are the First People, you know. The worm-children they call the Second People. I was a great puzzle to them at first, with my four limbs and my eyes that see, neither First nor Second. But I brought them flesh and learned their tongue, and so taught them of the Third People. You mock groun secrets, and in truth they are as rotting as you, yet they know things. They remember the Changemasters, their great enemies and the greatest friends of the *yaga-la-hai*, who wore the theta as a sigil, and in times long gone made the spiders and the worms and a thousand other things. Here, where I live, was where they sculptured and shaped the stuff of life, so the *yaga-la-hai* might live. Here they fashioned the bloodworms that still afflict the grouns, the light-hunger that drives them upward to their deaths if they catch it, and the huge white eaterworms that multiply and grow more terrible every day. You, all of you, have forgotten these things, but the Changemasters were gods greater than your White Worm could ever be. Grouns flinch before the theta. With good reason. The *yaga-la-hai* do not remember this room and the grouns had forgotten where it was, but I found it, and slowly I learn its secrets. I learned about your Manworm here. After the grouns had brought darkness to the burrows and killed most of the Changemasters, one was left. But he had lost all the runes, and he despaired. Still, he was the ruler. The *yaga-la-hai* followed him. And he remembered how worms, a thousand kinds of worms, had been men's best weapons against the grouns, and he knew how worms flourished better down here than men. So the last Changemaster trained the surgeon-priests in a few arts and had himself made into a great worm. Then he died. You see? He wanted to fashion the Third People. He was a Changemaster, but a poor one, an animal. Since then, all the leaders of the *yaga-la-hai* are fashioned into worms. But no

Third People exist. Until now. As I learn more Changemaster secrets, I will shape the Third People, and they will not be like the Manworm."

"You will shape nothing," Groff said. He started forward, and torchlight ran up and down the sharp-honed blade of his ax.

"Oh?" said the Meatbringer. And suddenly he reached out, and seized the two great doors on either side of him, and swung them shut behind him, ducking beneath the whistling blade of Groff's ax in the same fluid motion. The doors came together with a great rending clang.

Darkness.

And the Meatbringer.

Laughing.

Annelyn thrust wildly into the black with his rapier, at the spot where the Meatbringer had been last. Nothing. He pierced air. "Riess," he called, frantic. "The torch, our *torch.*" He heard Groff's ax swing again, and there was a jarring of metal, and a scream. A match blazed briefly; Riess, wide-eyed, held it in cupped hnds. Then, before Annelyn could even get his bearings, a knife flashed in the small circle of flame and Riess's round face disintegrated in a rush of blood and the match was falling and there was darkness again and laughing. The Meatbringer, the Meatbringer. Annelyn stood blind and helpless, rapier in limp fingers. Riess dead and Groff he didn't know and the Meatbringer laughing and *he* was next, he Annelyn, and *he couldn't see . . .*

The air duct was behind him. He dropped the rapier, stepped back, fumbled for the rope in the shaft. In the darkness, a sound like a butcher cutting meat; thick fleshy chopping, and groans. Annelyn found the rope and swung out, started to climb. Something grabbed his ankle. He reached down with one hand to yank loose the grip and suddenly the other hand couldn't support him, and he was falling, *falling*, with one hand still on the rope and his palm burning, *falling*, plunging into infinite black. He threw his body back and smashed against one wall of the shaft, sliding a few feet as his knees came up and he wedged himself in painfully and took a firmer hold on the rope. Then he had it again, by both hands.

A chill went through him. The Meatbringer was up above him now. And he remembered what Groff had said, about cutting the rope. The Meatbringer would cut the rope. He would fall forever.

He kicked, and his foot met only metal. As fast as he could he began to descend, hand under hand, down in total darkness, kicking every foot of the way. Finally his foot swung free; a new level, and the grid was gone!

He swung out and lay panting on the floor. He was a blind man now, he thought, and shuddered. Then he remembered. Matches. He had matches. All of them, he and Vermyllar and Riess, all of them had brought plenty of matches. But Riess had their torch.

Annelyn listened carefully. There was no noise from the shaft. He stood, his hand still shaking, and fumbled until he found his match box, his beautiful carved match box of fine metal and wood. He struck a match, and leaned into the air duct.

The rope was gone.

He moved his hand back and forth, just to be certain. But

the rope was gone. Cut, no doubt, and fallen silently. He had no way of knowing how close he had come . . . but the Meatbringer would know. The Meatbringer would know exactly where Annelyn was right now. And he would be coming.

The match burned his fingers. Startled, he blew it out, tossing it smoking down the shaft. Then he stood thinking.

The rope was cut. That meant — that meant there was no doubt left; the Meatbringer had won, Groff was dead up above. Yes. That meant there was no way back. No, wait. It only meant that *that* way back was closed, unless the Meatbringer dropped a new rope, and Annelyn could not guess when or if that would happen. But there must be other ways up, ways that passed by the Meatbringer's level and the Chamber of the Changemasters, as the Meatbringer had called them. He had to try to find his way up. He didn't remember the exact way they'd come — Groff had been right, yes — but he could tell up from down, and that might be enough. He had to start, before the Meatbringer found him. Yes.

First, he needed a torch.

He lit another match, held it high, and in its brief flicker looked around. A bronze fist, fingerless and torchless, was just above his head to one side of the air duct. He could see little else; the match gave scant light. Then it went out, and there was no light at all again.

Annelyn considered. No doubt he would find another fist a few feet from this one, and another a few feet from that. One of them might have a torch he could use. He began to walk, one hand clutching his matches tightly, the other patting the unseen wall to make sure it was still there. When he thought he had come far enough, he struck another match. And saw another empty fist.

After he had wasted four of his matches, he tried a new method. He pocketed his match box and began to grope very carefully down the wall, *feeling* for the fists. He found eight of them that way, and a sharp stump of metal that cut his hand and had probably been a ninth. Each of them was empty, corroded. Finally, in despair, he sank to the floor.

There would be no torches. He had come too deep. Down here, though the *yaga-la-hai* had held these burrows once, the grouns had ruled for endless ages. They hated torches. It was hopeless. Up in the Undertunnel, yes, and even in the border regions, the so-called groun-runs, yes. But not here.

Yet, without a torch — his matches were next to useless. They would never lead him out.

Perhaps he could make a torch, Annelyn thought. He tried to recall how torches were made. The shafts were generally wood. The crooked ones were cut from the bent yellow bloodfruit tree, after the leaves and the red-white berries had been put into the breeding tanks for the foodworms. And then there were the straight ones, longer and white, the shafts made by binding together thick strips from the stem of a giant mushroom and soaking them in — what? something — until they were hard. And then something was wrapped around the end. A cloth, soaked in something-or-other, or a greasy bag of dry fungus, or something. That was what burned. But he didn't know the details. Besides, without a torch, how could he find a bloodfruit tree or a giant mushroom? And how could he find the right fungus, and dry it, if that was what you were supposed to do? No. He could not make a torch, no more than he could find one.

Annelyn was frightened. He began to shake. Why was he down here, why, *why*? He could be up among the *yaga-la-hai*, in flamesilk and spidergray, bantering with Caralee or munching spiced spiders at a masque. Now, instead of munching, he was likely to be eaten. By the grouns, if they found him, or by the Meatbringer. He remembered vividly the way the Meatbringer had quaffed the cup full of Vermyllar's lifeblood.

The thought sent Annelyn to his feet. The Meatbringer would be coming for him. He must go somewhere, even if he could not see *where*. Frantic, with one hand he pulled loose his stiletto while with the other he felt for the reassuring wall, and he began to walk.

The burrow was endlessly black, and full of terrors. The wall was the only sanity, cool and firm beside him, with its fists and its air ducts where they should be. The rest — there were sounds around him, rustlings and scurryings, and he was never sure if he imagined them or not. Often, in the long walk toward nothing, he thought he heard the Meatbringer laughing, laughing just as he had at the Sun Masque so long ago. He heard it dimly and far-off, above him, below him, behind him. Once he heard it in front of him, and stopped, and held his breath and waited for an hour or perhaps a week without once moving, but there was no one there at all. After a time Annelyn saw lights too; vague shadowy shapes and drifting globes and crouching things that glowed and ran away. Or did he only think he saw them? They were always distant, or just around some bend, or glowing behind him and not there when he turned to see. He spied a dozen torches, off ahead of him, burning bright and crackling with hope, but each was snatched away or snuffed before he could run to it. He found only empty bronze fists, when he found anything at all.

He was walking very fast now, even running, and his footsteps echoed deafeningly, as if an army of the *yaga-la-hai* were trotting into battle. Annelyn didn't remember when he had begun to run; he was simply doing it, to keep ahead of the sounds, to reach the lights in front of him, and it seemed as if he had been doing it for a long while.

He had been running and running and running for what seemed like days when he lost the wall.

One moment his hand was on it, brushing the stone and the rusted teeth of the air-duct grills. Then nothing, and his hand was flailing in air, and he stumbled and fell.

It was dark. There were no lights. It was silent. There was no sound. The echoes had died. He was completely turned around. Where was he? What way had he been going? He had lost his knife.

He began to crawl, and finally he found the knife where it had dropped. Then he stood, his arms groping ahead of him, and walked toward where the wall should be. It wasn't there. He walked longer than he should have had to. Where had the wall gone? If this was only a junction, *something* should be there.

Annelyn had an idea. "Help!" he shouted, as loudly as he could. Echoes sounded, loud and then softer, bouncing, fading. His throat was very dry. He was not in a burrow. He had come out into some great chamber. He started to count his footsteps. He had reached three hundred, and lost count, when he finally came to a wall.

He felt it carefully, exploring it with his hands. It was very smooth; not stone at all, but some kind of metal. Parts of it were cool, others faintly warm, and there were one or two places — little spots no bigger than his fingernail — that seemed cold to the touch, almost icy. Annelyn decided to risk a match. Its brief flame showed him only a blank expanse of dull metal, stretching away to both sides of him. Nothing else. Nothing to indicate why some sections were warmer than others.

The match went out. Annelyn put the box away again, and began to follow the strange wall. The temperature patterns continued for a time, then stopped, then resumed again, then stopped. His footsteps echoed loudly. And his hand found no fists, no air ducts.

Exhausted at last, hoping that he had come far enough from the Meatbringer, he sank down to rest. He slept. And woke when something touched him.

The stiletto was beside him. Annelyn screamed and reached for it and struck all in the same instant, and he felt the blade cut something — cloth? Flesh? He didn't know. He was on his feet then, jabbing this way and that with his stiletto. Then, jumping around and whirling in circles, fighting vacant darkness, he began to fumble in his pocket for a match. He found one, and struck it.

The groun shrieked.

Annelyn saw it briefly in the light before it stepped back into the infinite black that surrounded him. A low crouching thing it was, covered by white skin and limp, colorless hair, dressed in gray rags. Its two rear limbs and one of its center pair were supporting it, and it was reaching for Annelyn with its two arms and the other center limb. Its arms and legs and the middle limbs, whatever you should call them, were all too long by a good foot, and too thin, and this particular groun was holding something in one of them, a net or something. Annelyn guessed what *that* was for. Its eyes were the worst thing, because they weren't eyes at all; they were pits in the face where eyes should be, soft, dark, moist pits that somehow let the grouns see in total darkness.

Annelyn faced the groun for less than a second, then jumped forward, swinging the stiletto and throwing the match at the creature. But the groun was already gone, after one short shriek and a moment of indecision. He could imagine it circling him, getting ready to cast that net, seeing everything he did although he could see nothing. He danced around inanely, trying to face all directions at once, and he lit another match. Nothing. Then he froze, hoping to hear the groun and stab it. Nothing. Grouns had big, soft, padded feet, he remembered, and they moved very softly.

Annelyn began to run.

He had no idea where he was going, but he had to *go.* He could not fight the groun, not without a torch or some light to see by, and it would get him if he stood still, but maybe he could outrun it. After all, he had hurt it with that first stab.

He ran through the darkness, his knife in one pumping fist, praying to the White Worm that he would not run into a wall, or the Meatbringer or a groun. He ran until he was breathless again. And then, quite suddenly, there was no floor beneath him.

He fell, screaming. Then the darkness drew deeper, deeper, and Annelyn had not even fear to light his way.

He had nothing at all.

He and Vermyllar were standing together outside the great iron doors to the High Burrow of the Manworm. Groff was there too, death-still in his bronze armor, standing the ancient guard. But on the other side of the chamber doors no knight stood, only a huge stuffed groun. It was twice the size of an ordinary groun, hideous and white, its two upper limbs frozen in a menacing, grasping pose.

"A horrible thing," Vermyllar said, shuddering.

Annelyn smiled at him. "Ah," he said lightly, "but so easy to make it beautiful!"

Vermyllar frowned. "No. what are you talking of, Annelyn? You can't make a groun beautiful. My grandfather was a son of the Manworm, and I know. There is no way."

"Nonsense," said Annelyn. "It is simple. To make a groun supremely beautiful, cover him."

"Cover him?"

"Yes. With mushroom sauce."

And Vermyllar grimaced, then chuckled despite himself, and it was a very fine moment. Except . . . except . . . just then the big groun came alive and chased them down the tunnel and ate Vermyllar, while Annelyn fled screaming.

The grouns were all around him, closing in slowly, their long thin arms groping and waving evilly as they advanced on him despite his torch. "No," Annelyn kept saying, "no, you can't come any farther, you can't, you are afraid of light." But the grouns, the eyeless blind grouns, paid no mind to his pleas or his torch. Then came in and in, crouching and swaying, moaning rhythmically. At the last moment, Annelyn remembered that he had a skin of mushroom sauce at his belt, which would surely scatter them in terror, since everyone knew how grouns felt about mushroom sauce. But before he could reach it to throw at them, the soft white hands had him, and he was being lifted and carried off into the darkness.

He was bound to a wheeled table, heavy metal shackles around his wrists and ankles, and there was pain, pain, horrible pain. He raised his head, slowly and with great difficulty, and saw that he was in the Chamber of the Changemasters. The Meatbringer, awash in the dim purplish illumination, was kneeling at the foot of the table, gnawing on his ankle. The cloak he wore looked strangely like Vermyllar.

The visions faded. Annelyn was in darkness once more. He lay on a rough floor of rocks and dust and dirt, and sharp pieces of stone were jabbing him uncomfortably in a hundred places. His ankle throbbed. He sat up, and touched it, and finally satisfied himself that it was only turned, not broken. Then he checked the rest of his body. The bones all seemed intact, and his matches were still there, thank the Worm. But his knife was gone, lost somewhere in the run or the fall.

Where was he?

He stood, and felt his head brush a low ceiling. His ankle screamed at him, and he shifted his weight to the other foot as much as he could, and put out a hand to lean against the wall. It was all soft and crumbly, disintegrating under his touch. This was an odd burrow, a burrow of dirt instead of stone or metal. And uneven — Annelyn groped ahead hesitantly, took a step or two, and found that both ceiling and floor were woefully irregular.

Where was he?

Somehow he had fallen down here, he remembered. There had been a hole in the floor of the immense chamber, and he had been running from the groun, and suddenly he was here. Perhaps the grouns had found him and carried him to this place, but that seemed unlikely. They would have killed him. No, more likely the hole had slanted at some point, and he had been knocked unconscious, and rolled down the slope. Something on that order. At any rate, there was no hole above his head now. Only dry, crumbling ceiling, and bits of rock that showered his head when he moved.

A new fear came to him then; this burrow was soft, so very soft and dry. What if it fell in on him? Then he would be truly trapped, with no way out, ever. But where could he go?

One thing was certain; he could not stay here. The air was hotter and thicker than he liked, and he had not noticed any air ducts in these dust-dry walls. And he was hungry, too. How long had he been down here? Was it only this morning that he and Riess and Vermyllar had set out down the Undertunnel? Or a week ago? When had he last eaten, or drunk? He wasn't sure.

Annelyn began to walk, limping and favoring his sore

ankle, feeling his way before him, crouching half the time when the ceiling dropped lower. Twice he hit his head on overhanging spears of stone, despite his careful progress. The bumps on his skull distracted him from his aching ankle.

Before long, the passage began to change. The walls, once dry, became faintly moist and then distinctly damp. But they remained soft — Annelyn could sink his fist into them, and squeeze the cool soil between his fingers. His boots sank deep into the floor with every step, and made squishing, sucking sounds when he pulled them free. But the air was no cleaner; it was growing thicker and more heavy and Annelyn had begun to consider reversing his direction. He thought he smelled something.

He decided to strike a match.

The flame burned for only a minute, but that was long enough for Annelyn. Something dark and feral chittered behind him, and he turned in time to see it briefly before it slid into the darkness: an eyeless furred shadow on many legs. There was a spiderweb hanging on a slant from roof to wall just behind him; he had broken it in passing with a clumsy, wandering hand. The spider was absent, perhaps eaten by some other denizen of the burrow. The walls on both sides of him were pockmarked by what looked like wormholes of all sizes. He lifted one foot, and saw that his boot was covered by a dozen small gray slugs, busily trying to chew through the tough leather. Before his match guttered out, Annelyn had plucked most of them free. They clung and made soft pops when he pulled them loose, and he crushed them between thumb and forefinger. Then he ate them. The taste was bitter, nothing like the subtle flavor of the fat slugs the *yaga-la-hai* served at their masques, and Annelyn reflected dourly that they might well poison him. But he was hungry, and the juices moistened his dusty throat.

His match burned out, and Annelyn decided to proceed forward. Here, at least, he had found life; behind him was only dry death. He could always turn around later if the air became much worse.

And it did become worse, as did the smell, which soon filled the burrow with a cloying sweetness that had Annelyn close to gagging. The sweetness of rot; ahead of him, something was dead in the tunnel.

He stumbled on, blind, wrinkling up his nose and trying to breathe through his mouth. He prayed to the White Worm that he could get past whatever had died.

Then he stepped in it.

One moment he was walking in damp clinging soil; the next, he felt something leathery split under his boot and he was ankle deep in mush and viscous liquid. The odor assaulted him with renewed vigor, fresh and horribly strong. Annelyn retched up the slugs he had just eaten and reeled backward, pulling free his foot.

When he had finished heaving, he leaned against the burrow wall, holding his nose, gasping, and with his free hand he found and struck a match. Then he bent forward, to see what it was. His hand was unsteady; he could hardly see anything but the match flame at first. He came closer.

The White Worm himself lay rotting in the burrow.

Annelyn drew back, frightened, and the match went out. But he lit another and recovered his nerve. Before he was finished, he had used at least ten matches; each served to illuminate only a part of the long carcass.

The worm — it was not the White Worm after all, Annelyn finally decided, though it was certainly bigger than anything *he'd* ever encountered — was far gone in its decay, past the peak of its ripeness, for which Annelyn was profoundly grateful. Even the ghost of its putrefaction was bad enough. Though shrunken in death, it filled the burrow three-quarters full, so that Annelyn had to hug the wall to squeeze by it. A thousand lesser worms and other wriggling things had feasted on its immense corpse, and a few still remained; Annelyn could see them crawling around inside, through the great worm's milky translucent skin.

The skin was part of the terror. Most of the monster's meat had decomposed into noxious fluids or had been consumed by the scavengers, but the skin was intact. It was like thick leather, cracked and brittle now, but still formidable. Not easy for an enemy to cut through. That was part of the terror, yes.

The mouth was another part. Annelyn saw it briefly by matchlight, and wasted a second match to be sure. It had teeth. Rings of them, five concentric rings each narrower than the one before, in a circular mouth large enough to swallow a man's head and shoulders. The inner rings were bone, ordinary bone, and that was bad enough, but the outermost ring, the greatest — the teeth were bluish black, glinting like . . . like . . . metal?

That was the second part of the terror.

The final part was its size. Annelyn measured it, match by

match, step by step, struggling to get by, struggling not to choke. The worm was at least twenty feet long.

He wasted no more matches when the corpse was behind him. He plunged forward as quickly as he could, blundering noisily through the dark until the smell was only an unpleasant memory and he could breathe again. Sometime during his rush forward, Annelyn realized why this burrow was so strange. A wormhole. He giggled insanely. It must be a wormhole.

When the blackness was once again a *clean* blackness, he slowed down. There was nothing to do but continue onward, after all.

He was remembering something strange the Meatbringer had said when he had been babbling about the Changemasters. Something about "huge white eaterworms, who multiply and grow more terrible every day." It hadn't made any particular sense then. Now, now it did. The Meatbringer had been talking to the Changemasters, of things they brought into the world to afflict the grouns. The thing that lay behind him was indeed an affliction. For the first time in his life, Annelyn felt sorrow for the grouns.

The burrow turned. He felt ahead of him and followed it around.

Then Annelyn saw a light.

He blinked, but it did not vanish; it was a small thing, a purplish glow so dark it almost blended with the blackness, but by now his eyes were very sharp for any trace of light at all. Not hurrying, he began to walk toward it, never daring to hope.

The light did not fade. It swelled as he drew nearer, growing steadily larger though scarcely any brighter. He could see nothing by it, nothing but the light itself, so dim was its glow.

After a time he saw that it was round. The end of the burrow. The wormhole came out somewhere.

When it had grown to man size and was still there, only then did Annelyn take heart and begin to tremble. He ran the last few feet, to the glowing violet circle of freedom, the magic portal that would restore his vision. He held the burrow walls with both hands as he looked through, and down.

Then he was very still indeed.

Below him was a huge chamber, bigger than the Chamber of the Changemasters. His wormhole had come out high above the floor, a round gap in a hard stone wall. He could see a hundred other wormholes with a glance, and things moving in some of them, and he could imagine a hundred others. The ceiling, the walls, the floor, all were covered by thick fungus, like that in the Meatbringer's throne room. Purple, purple, thick as a haze and ominous; the room was suffused with the vague glow of the omnipresent growth.

Annelyn barely noticed it.

There was a great tank, too, full of some liquid, and globes in the ceiling that dripped some other substance, and air ducts where ropes of fungus swayed in the hot breeze, but Annelyn took little note of them. He was watching the worms.

Eaterworms. Giants, forty feet long, smaller ones like the corpse he had encountered, dead ones, and a million writhing younglings. The chamber was a nest of eaterworms, a breeding tank and nursery for the monsters. But not a prison.

Not for creatures that could chew through stone, not for these nightmares with translucent flesh and iron teeth. Annelyn made the sign of the worm, then realized what he had done, and giggled. He was a dead man.

He stood despairing while shadowy shapes slid through the moist purple bloom beneath him.

But at last he began to think again. None of the things seemed to be coming toward him. He had escaped their notice, at least for now, and that fanned his tiny fire of hope. He would use whatever moments were left to him. His eyes strained, as he studied the bowllike chamber.

Dimly, across the room, he saw lines running up and down the walls, bulging beneath the fungus, crossing on the ceiling, branching from the globes. Pipes, he thought, water pipes. The *yaga-la-hai* knew water pipes. But the knowledge was useless to him.

Other shapes, made vague and hulking by distance and growth, sat still on the floor. The worms moved over them, between them. Annelyn thought he saw metal, overgrown by purple, but he lost it quickly. No matter; it would do him no good.

On the curve of the right-hand wall, he could make out a gleam beneath a coat of fungus. His eyes followed it. There were outlines. More pipes? No. There was a design. It came clear. It was a theta, with wormholes all around it.

Annelyn touched the golden theta enbroidered on his breast. Perhaps *that* was why the eaterworms had not attacked him. What was it that the Meatbringer had said? That the Changemasters had shaped the great worms and other horrors, that the Changemasters wore the theta, that they were the best champions of the *yaga-la-hai* and the worst enemies of the grouns. . . . Could it be that the monsters ate only grouns? That they thought *him* a Changemaster, and thus left him alone?

Annelyn couldn't believe it. A few strings of golden thread could not possibly stay those things. Annelyn looked at the right-hand wall again, then dismissed the subject from his mind.

He continued his examination of the murky chamber. And, one by one, he found the exits.

There were three of them, one on each wall. A fourth one, perhaps, lay below him, but the angle made it impossible to see. The doors to each were double, and they looked metallic. The one to the right was the closest; it lay just under the theta shape. He could make out its details, very faintly. He saw shafts, thick bars of metal running across the door, blocking it. Bolts.

Rusted in place, he thought. For how long? Impossible to move. Yet, what other answer was there? All the other ways out were wormholes; even those that looked vacant would be groun-black just a few feet away from this chamber. He would risk blundering into an eaterworm in the darkness. Anything would be better than that.

But if he stayed here, eventually he would starve, or the worms would finally notice him. He had to go either forward or back.

He knew what lay behind. The dead worm's hole was safe enough, but beyond it lay only the vast chamber and the grouns, the infinite empty blackness. He could never find the tunnel that had led him there. He would never get back.

Annelyn sighed. He had been so long in darkness. He was tired, and conscious of a change that lay like a weight on his shoulders. He had forgotten the Meatbringer and the question of revenge. He was doomed, no matter what he did. The grouns, the Changemasters, the Third People — what difference did any of it make?

Once, at a half-remembered masque, he had called himself a freethinker. But now the ancient worship words came back to him, the mockingly obscure rote that the Manworm had intoned so often, so wearily. It had always seemed odd, in parts meaningless. But now the phrases seemed to speak to him; they danced macabre dances in his head, and came bubbling to his lips. In a hopeless voice, he began to mouth them, very quietly, much as Riess (old fat dead Riess) might have done in his place.

"That White Worm has many names," he said, unmoving, "and the children of men have cursed them all in the centuries behind us. But we are the worm-children, and we do not curse them. He cannot be fought. His is the final power in the universe, and the wise man accepts his coming, to dance and feast in what time there is left.

"So praise the White Worm, whose name is Yaggalla. And grieve not, though our lights burn dim and die.

"So praise the White Worm, whose name is Decay. And grieve not, though our energy fades and fails.

"So praise the White Worm, whose name is Death. And grieve not, though life's circle tightens and all things perish.

"So praise the White Worm, whose name is Entropy. And grieve not, though the sun goes out.

"An ending comes. Feast. The ships are gone. Drink. The

struggling times are over. Dance. And praise, praise, to the White Worm."

Silence; Annelyn eyed the long, pale wrigglers moving below. How foolish it was to prolong things. The struggling times were over. He would go forward.

He tried to grab a handhold in the fungus that fringed his wormhole, but there was no strength to it, and it ripped free in his hand. So nothing remained but to jump, and hope that his legs would not crack and splinter, hope that the beckoning carpet below would prove as comforting as it looked. Annelyn turned and lowered himself; he looked down past his feet, and when the floor seemed clear enough of writhing life, he dropped.

And landed jarringly, though he tried to flex his legs under him. The growth was thick, layers on layers, waist deep; it softened his fall, but it also sent his feet skidding out from under him, and he tripped and fell in a tangle of purple threads. When he rose, on edge but unhurt, bits of glowing fungus clung to his burrow-black clothing.

Abruptly his immunity ended. A worm the size of his leg slid toward him, its mouth rippling rhythmically. Annelyn kicked free and brought his boot down on the attacker, as savagely as he could. His damaged ankle reminded him forcefully that he should not be doing such things. But the worm was forced down through the living purple mat and squashed against the floor. Its skin did not seem as thick or as strong as that of its larger cousins.

Other worms were moving beneath the fungus, pale writhings that Annelyn barely saw. One of the giants had noticed him now; it moved toward him, over the sleeping body of another. Annelyn glanced around hurriedly; worms were converging from all sides.

But the wall was only a few feet away. And the fourth door, the one he had prayed would be there. It was shut and overgrown like the others, but he would not have to walk on a hundred worms to reach it.

He struggled over to it, and felt a sharp jolt of pain just as he collapsed against the metal. A small eaterworm was boring into his thigh. Annelyn ripped it loose, whirled it around his head, and flung it spinning across the length of the chamber, to splatter on the side of the large tank. He turned back to the exit, and wildly began to rip loose fungus. There were three bolts. With the heel of his hand he hammered upward at the topmost bolt, once, twice, three times, and the heavy metal shaft finally moved an inch. Another smash, and the rust that had welded it to its brackets gave; it came free in his hands.

He turned, holding the length of metal like a club, and brought it down hard on the nearest of the eaterworms. The blow broke skin, but barely, barely; it was an old worm, as large as Annelyn. It oozed, and turned aside, colliding with one slightly larger. It did not die.

He could not fight them. He swung the club once more, then went back to the door. The middle bolt came free after three sharp knocks. The lowest shaft proved an illusion; it disintegrated into flakes of fungus-eaten rust when Annelyn wrapped his hands around it. Frantic, he pounded at the length of metal between the brackets until it fell apart, and the door was free. Something bit him. He screamed and pulled at the handles, and they came loose in his hands, but the door moved only a fraction of an inch. Then he scrabbled madly with his fingers, tearing loose a nail, wedging his hands into the slim black crack until he had purchase. He could *feel* the monsters behind him. With all his strength, he pulled backward.

The hinges screamed, the metal creaked, while fungus worked against him to keep the door shut. But it moved, it *moved*! An inch, two, then six all at once. That was enough for Annelyn. He flattened himself and held his breath and squeezed through, into the quiet dark beyond. Then he threw himself to the floor, rolling over and over and thrashing up and down, until the worm that had clung to him was only a slimy paste that coated his clothes.

When he got up, he struck a match. He did not look back at the purple hell beyond the narrow opening he had forced.

He was in a very small chamber, solid metal, round, dark. Before him was another door, also of metal, and round. In its center was a wheel.

His match went out. Fungus still hung from his besoiled garments and his fine blond hair, and more was scattered on the floor, glowing dimly. Annelyn pulled at the wheel. Nothing. He tried turning it, but it would not move. Beside it was a metal bar, in a slit. That refused to move also, until he put all his weight on it and forced it down. Then he could turn the wheel, though it spun slowly and with difficulty.

Annelyn was drenched in sweat, and the metal was moist with the wetness of his palms. But it was not rusted, he suddenly realized. It was dark and strong and cool, like something newly pulled from the forges of the bronze knights.

Hissing suddenly began, all around him. He stopped,

startled, and looked over his shoulder, but none of the eater-worms had yet squeezed through, so he went back to the wheel. When it would turn no more, he pulled, and the door swung smoothly outward on its huge hinges. The hissing grew louder, and Annelyn was buffeted by a tremendous gush of moist air, rushing forward from behind him.

Then he was through, pulling the door shut. It was pitch-dark again; the little fungus fragments that hung on him became worms' eyes in the blackness. But better this than risk the chamber of the eaterworms again.

His matches again. The match box rattled despairingly when Annelyn shook it. He counted the remaining matches by feeling with his fingers. A dozen left, if that; his fingers kept losing track, and he might have counted the same match twice. He chose one, grateful for its brief light.

He was standing less than a foot from a groun.

Annelyn moved, backward, in a leap. There was no sound. He came forward again, holding the flame before him like a weapon. The groun was still there. Frozen. And there was something between them. He touched it. Glass. Feeling infinitely easier, he began to move the match up and down. He lit another, and explored further.

A whole wall of grouns!

Annelyn briefly considered trying to shatter the glass and eat one of the imprisoned grouns, but discarded the idea. They were clearly stuffed; they had probably been here for more years than he had lived. And they were unusual grouns, at that. Males and females alternated, and each in the long row was partially flayed, a section of its skin peeled back to reveal inside. A different section on each groun, at that.

There were also statues of grouns and groun skulls, and a six-limbed skeleton. The last groun was the most singular. Though colorless, its garments were as fine and rich as any of the *yaga-la-hai.* On its head was a metal helmet, such as a bronze knight might wear, all of black metal with a thin red window curving around the front for its eyes. And it held something, pointing it. A tube of some sort, fashioned of the same black metal as the helmet. Strangest of all, both helmet and tube were emblazoned with silver thetas.

Annelyn used four of his matches examining the row of grouns, hoping to find something that would help him. He had so few left, but it was foolish to hoard them now. Finding nothing, he crossed the room, groping for the other wall. He tripped over a table, went around it, and collided with another. They were both empty. Finally he felt glass again.

This wall was full of worms.

Like the grouns, they were dead, or stuffed, or cased in the glass; Annelyn did not care which it was, so long as they did not move. A four-foot-long eaterworm dominated the display, but there were dozens of others as well. Most of them were unknown to him, though he had eaten worms all his life. They had one thing in common: they looked dangerous. A lot of them had teeth, which Annelyn found very disquieting. A few wore what looked like stings in their tails.

He explored the rest of the chamber; it was long and narrow, sheathed in metal, seemingly untouched by time, and capped by a large, wheeled door at each end. A lot of tables were scattered about, and metal chairs, but nothing of interest to Annelyn. Once he came across something shaped like a torch, but the shaft was metal and the head glass, totally useless. Perhaps he could fill the glass part with the glowing fungus, he thought. He tucked the instrument under his arm. Other things he found as well, bulking pillars and shapes of metal and glass, vaguely like those he had seen shattered on the edge of the bridge in the Chamber of the Last Light, and in the Meatbringer's throne room. He could not fathom their purpose.

At length, his matches all but exhausted, he went back to the wall of the grouns. Something was nagging at him, pulling at the back of his brain. He looked again at the last groun in the row, then at the tube. That was being held almost like a weapon, Annelyn decided. And it bore a theta. It might be useful. He took the metal shaft of the thing-that-was-almost-a-torch, and smashed at the thick glass with a series of sharp blows. It cracked and cracked and cracked some more, but did not shatter. Finally, when his arm had begun to ache, Annelyn ripped through with his hands, clawing aside splinters of not-quite-glass that still hung maddeningly together. He grabbed the groun's tube, and began to play with its various bars and handles.

A few minutes later, he discarded it with disgust. Useless, whatever it had been.

Something still bothered him. He lit another match and considered the helmeted groun. A wrongness there . . .

It hit him. The helmet, the reddish window. But a groun had no eyes! Annelyn widened the gap he had made in the glasslike wall, and lifted the helmet from the dead groun's head.

This groun had eyes.

He moved his match very close. Eyes, all right; small and

black, sunk deep in moist sockets, but definitely eyes. Yet this groun was the only eyed groun in the wall; the next one down, a heavy female, was eveless, as were all the rest.

His match died. Annelyn tried on the helmet.

Light was all around him.

He shouted, whirled, bobbed his head up and down. He could see! He could see the whole room, in a glance! Without a match, or a torch! He could see!

The walls were glowing, very faintly, smoky red. The metal pillars — eight of them, he saw now — were bright orange, though the other metallic shapes remained shadowed. The doors were dark, but yellowish light leaked around the edge of the one he had come through. It pulsed. The very air seemed to give a dim light, a ghostly glow that Annelyn found hard to pin down. The dead grouns and the worms opposite stood in rows like soot-gray statues, outlined by the illumination around them.

Annelyn's fingers found the theta on the crest of the helmet. He was wearing a rune of the Changemasters, clearly! But — but why had it been on a *groun*?

He considered the question for an instant, then decided that it did not matter. All that mattered was the helmet. He picked up his metal shaft again, a cool gray stick in the smoldering reddish chamber. The glass at its end had been broken into jagged shards by his efforts to smash through the window. That was fine. It would make an excellent weapon. Almost jauntily, Annelyn turned toward the far door.

The burrow beyond was dark, but it was a darkness he could deal with, a darkness he had dealt with every day of his life in the dimly lit tunnels of the *yaga-la-hai*; it was made of shadows and vague shapes and dust, not the total blackness he had wandered in since fleeing the Meatbringer. Of course, it was not really like that — once, hesitantly, he lifted the helmet and instantly went blind again — but he cared little, if he could see. And he *could* see. The cool stone walls were a faded red, the air faintly misty and alight, and the ducts he passed were orange-edged maws that spewed streams of reddish smoke out into the burrows, to curl and rise and dissipate.

Annelyn walked down the empty tunnel, for once imagining no sights and hearing no noises. He came to branchings several times and each time chose his way arbitrarily. He found shadowed stairways and climbed them eagerly, as far up as they would take him. Twice he detoured uneasily around the man-sized, dimly radiant pits he recognized as wormholes; one other time, he glimpsed a live eaterworm — a sluggishly moving river of smoke-dark ice — crossing a junction up ahead of him. Annelyn's own body, seen through the helmet, glowed a cheerful orange. The bits of fungus that still hung from his tattered clothing were like chunks of yellow fire.

He had been walking for an hour when he first encountered a live groun. It was less bright than he himself, a six-limbed specter of deep red, a radiant wraith seen down a side burrow out of the corner of his eye. But soon Annelyn observed that it was following him. He began to walk closer to the wall, feeling his way as if he were blind, and the groun who ghosted him grew more bold. It was a large one, Annelyn observed, cloth hanging from it like a flapping second skin, a net trailing from one hand, a knife in the other.

He wondered briefly if it could be the same groun he had met before.

When he reached a stairway, a narrow spiral between two branching corridors, Annelyn paused, fumbled, and turned. The groun came straight on toward him, lifting its knife, padding very quietly on its soft feet. Oddly, Annelyn discovered that he was not afraid. He would smash in its head as soon as it crept close enough.

He lifted his glass-edged club. The groun came nearer. Now he could kill it. Except, except — somehow he didn't want to. "Stop, groun," he said instead. He was not quite sure why.

The groun froze, edged backward. It said something in a low guttural moan. Annelyn understood nothing of it. "I hear you," he said, "and I see you, groun. I am wearing a rune of the Changemasters." He pointed at the theta stitched in gold on his breast.

The groun gibbered in terror, dropped its net, and began to run. Annelyn ruefully decided that he ought not to have drawn attention to his theta. On impulse, he decided to follow the groun; perhaps, in its fear, it would lead him to an exit. If not, he could always find his way back to the stair.

He pursued it down three corridors, around two turns, before he lost sight of it entirely. The groun had been running very quickly, while Annelyn was still getting an occasional twinge from his ankle, making it difficult to keep up. Yet he continued on after the groun had vanished, hoping to pick up the trail again.

Then the creature reappeared, running *toward* him. It saw him, stopped, glanced back over a shoulder. Then, seemingly determined, it resumed its headlong, four-legged gallop, one of its remaining limbs brandishing its knife.

Annelyn flourished his club, but the groun did not slow. Then inspiration struck. He reached into his pocket, and produced his last match.

The groun shrieked, and four long legs began to scrabble madly on the burrow floor as it skidded to a halt. But it was not the only one surprised. Annelyn himself, dazzled by the coruscating brilliance that seemed to stab into his brain, choked and staggered and dropped the match. Both of them stood blinking.

But something else moved. A cold gray shadow was drifting down onto the groun, filling the tunnel like a wall of mist. The front of it rippled in and out, in and out, in and out.

Annelyn shook his head, and the eaterworm loomed clear.

Without thought, he jumped forward, swinging his club over the head of the groun. The blow glanced harmlessly off the worm's leathery skin. Then Annelyn drew back, kicked the groun to get it moving, and thrust his glass-edged pole into the contracting mouth of the attacker.

He was running then, the groun next to him, darting around narrow turns until he was certain that they'd lost the worm. They retraced their old footsteps, and the narrow stair appeared in their path.

The groun stopped, and swung to face him. Annelyn stood with empty hands.

The groun raised its knife, then cocked its head to one side. Annelyn matched the motion. That seemed to satisfy the creature. It sheathed the blade, squatted in the dust thick on the burrow floor, and began to sketch a map.

The groun's finger left glowing trails that lingered for a time, then faded rapidly. But the symbols it used meant nothing to Annelyn. "No," he said, shaking his head. "I cannot follow."

The groun looked up. Then it rose, gestured, and started up the stair, glancing back to see if Annelyn was behind it. He was.

They climbed that stair and another, walked through a series of wide burrows, pulled themselves up rust-eaten ladders through narrow wells. Then came more tunnels, the groun looking back periodically, Annelyn following docilely. He was nervous, but he kept telling himself that the groun *could* have killed him before; surely if that had been what it intended, it would have done so by now.

Other grouns moved through the burrows. Annelyn saw one, a skeletal red shape with a long sword and one missing limb, and then two together with knives crouching near a junction. They gave him ominous eyeless looks. Later, they passed whole crowds of grouns, some of them in long garments that dragged on the floor and shone softly in many colors. All gave him a wide berth. He saw wormholes, too, most dark and cold, others ringed by faint halos that sent chills up his spine.

After more climbing and turning than Annelyn cared to remember, they came out into a large chamber. A dozen grouns sat over smoking bowls at long metal tables, shoveling food into their mouths. They regarded him impassively.

Annelyn caught the scent of food — a fungus mush, torchtenders' food — and was suddenly, ravenously hungry. But no one offered him a bowl. His guide spoke to another groun seated near the center of the table, a grossly fat individual with an enormous, misshapen head. Finally the huge groun — he must have weighed more than Groff, Annelyn thought — shoved aside his bowl of steaming food, rose, and came over to Annelyn. His head moved up and down, up and down, as he inspected the intruder. Four soft hands began to pat him all over, and Annelyn gritted his teeth and tried not to flinch. It wasn't as bad as he had expected. He found himself regarding the new groun almost like a person, instead of a thing.

The fat groun cocked his head to one side. Annelyn remembered and did the same. The groun joined four hands together in a huge fist, raised it, lowered it. Annelyn, with only two hands, did his best to mimic the gesture.

Then the groun held up one finger, and jabbed at his own chest with another hand. Annelyn started to imitate him, but the groun restrained him. This was something more than a vision test. Annelyn was still.

The groun held up two fingers on a hand of an upper limb, his two middle limbs went out to either side, and his great body shook. His opposing upper arm came up, and *that* hand flashed three fingers. The groun looked from one hand to the other and back again, then repeated the gesture. He looked at Annelyn, and was still.

Annelyn glanced from the groun's upper right hand — two fingers — to the upper left — three. The Meatbringer's words returned to him. He raised his own hand, and spread three fingers.

The groun lowered all his hands, and again the immense body quivered. He turned back to another of his kind, and they spoke together in their soft, mournful way. Annelyn could not follow their talk, but he hoped he had made himself understood.

Finally the leader turned and walked back around the table, seated himself, and returned to his bowl of fungus. Annelyn's erstwhile guide took him by the elbow, and beckoned him to follow. They went together from the chamber. The groun began leading him upward once more.

As they walked on and on, climbing one ladder after another and ascending stairways only to descend others, wandering through long burrows full of grouns shuffling and muttering, Annelyn grew increasingly conscious of his exhaustion. Whatever magic had kept him functioning until now was rapidly wearing off — his ankle hurt, his thigh hurt, his hands hurt, he was starved and parched and filthy, and he badly needed rest and sleep. But the groun showed no mercy, and Annelyn could only strive to keep up with his rapid pace.

Afterward, of all the burrows they passed through, only a few pictures lingered in his memory.

One time, the two of them walked down a narrow passage that was frightfully, eerily cold; the gloom was thick enough to cut, and Annelyn saw pipes, intensely black and throbbing, along the low ceiling. Wisps of ebony fog curled around them, then fell like slow streamers to the floor; Annelyn and the groun walked boot deep in chilled black mist. Under the pipes, wicked metal hooks curved outward. Most of them were empty, but two held the carcasses of rope-thin worms of a kind Annelyn had never encountered. A third held poor fat Riess, naked and dead, an obscene carving of obsidian, with a hook in the back of his neck so he dangled grotesquely. Annelyn started to make the sign of the worm, stopped himself, and shuffled by. If he had held up two fingers instead of three, he suspected, he might now occupy the hook right next to his one-time friend.

Two other chambers struck him forcefully, for both were among the largest open spaces he had ever seen. The first of these was so hot that sweat ran down his arms, while the orange glare of the air stung his eyes. It was a room so large he could barely see the far side. Pipes were everywhere, thick and thin, some strangely dark and others brilliant, like metal worms running over floor and walls and ceilings. The vast spaces above were filled by a web of thin bridges and ropes: up there, Annelyn glimpsed a thousand grouns, limber on six legs and born to the air, scampering up and down and around on the web, turning wheels and pushing bars, tending five immense shapes of metal that stood several levels high and burned with stabbing white light. His guide led him through the chamber on ground level, detouring through the maze of pipes, while the other grouns swung by and paid them little attention.

The second chamber, three levels higher and long minutes later, was just as huge, but desolate. No light here, no shapes of metal, no ropes or bridges; and the only groun Annelyn saw here was a lone, armed hunter who stood like a tiny red bug in the far distance across the room, and watched them as they passed. The floor and the walls were stone, dusty and dry and melancholy, but in places they were lined by a metal paneling that shone faintly with lights of many different hues. When Annelyn and his guide walked near one of these, he saw that a picture was glowing on the panel. It was an intricate, labored depiction of sword-swinging grouns battling a giant whose eyes were thetas and whose fingers were worms. He had to look hard and long to make sense of the scene, however; as with the tapestries of the *yaga-la-hai*, here too the colors were dim and fading, and rust had eaten black, flaking holes in some of the panels. One more thing Annelyn noted about the great, abandoned chamber: wormholes. The floor was full of them.

Afterward, they went straight for a long time. Annelyn noticed broken bronze fists on the walls then, and some of his weariness lifted. He was closer to home. The *yaga-la-hai* had lived here once.

Abruptly, the groun stopped. Annelyn stopped too.

They stood beside an air duct. It had no grill. Annelyn smiled wanly, leaned forward, and reached inside. His hand brushed rope.

The groun made an odd sweeping gesture, turned, and set off back the way he had come, moving rapidly on four limbs. Soon Annelyn was alone. He reached into the warm shaft, gripped the rope, and started to climb. This time he could see where he was going. The metal sides around him were a friendly reddish color, the air faintly misty and moving steadily upward, past him. When he was between levels, he could look up and down, and in both directions see the shadowed squares of exits.

He swung out one level up, and removed his helmet, cradling it under his arm. The great metal doors hung open. Annelyn stood in shadows, and let his eyes adjust to the pale, purple gloom. The fungus-encrusted globes still shone in the

Chamber of the Changemasters, but the torches had been snuffed. Of the Meatbringer, he saw no sign. He waited until he was sure, then went inside.

The first thing he took up was a weapon. His own rapier was there, on top of a pile of rusting blades, and he reclaimed it with satisfaction. He tested Groff's great ax, lying up against the throne, but found it too heavy and awkward. Instead, he slid Vermyllar's dagger into his belt, and Riess's into a boot. If he were to blood the Meatbringer, it seemed appropriate to use those tools.

Then he wandered around the chamber, picking at things, exploring, searching for food. He finally found a cache of meat, strips salted and hung. Plenty of good white grounmeat, and some other kind as well. But Annelyn found he could eat none of it. He settled for a bowl of spiced spiders and a plate of mushrooms.

After eating, he rested on one of the wheeled beds, too tired to sleep, and too frightened. Instead, he scrutinized a book he had found lying open beside the throne. Its covers were heavy leather, impressed with the theta and a row of symbols, but the pages inside had not endured the long passage of time as well. Some were missing entirely, others were damp and overgrown by paper mold, and the few fragments still legible made no sense to Annelyn. The symbols were vaguely like the writing in the crumbling libraries kept by the Manworm; Annelyn had learned to read a little of it from Vermyllar, who in turn had learned the dark art from his grandfather. It did not help. He could puzzle out a word here, guess at one on the page following, and yet another, ten chapters on, but never two words together that made sense. Even the pictures were meaningless tangles of lines, depicting nothing that he recognized.

Annelyn set the book aside. Noises were coming from the air duct. He stood, took his helmet and rapier, and went outside the chamber doors to wait.

The Meatbringer emerged from the shaft, dressed in white grounskin with a colorless cloak. Ropes of spidersilk bound the body of a small male child to his back. The boy was of the *yaga-la-hai*.

Annelyn stepped forward.

The Meatbringer looked up, startled. He had begun to untie the knots that held his prey. Now his hand went to his knife. "So," he said. "You."

"Me," said Annelyn. His rapier was extended, his helmet cradled by his free hand.

"I searched for you," the Meatbringer said. "After I hung a new rope."

"I fled," said Annelyn, "knowing that you would search."

"Yes," the Meatbringer said, smiling. His knife came out, a whisper of metal on leather. "I feared you were lost. This is better. The grouns pay well for meat. Your friends, by the way, were delicious. Except for the knight. Unfortunately, he was quite tough."

"I wonder how you will taste," Annelyn said.

The Meatbringer laughed.

"I suspect your flesh would be foul," Annelyn continued. "I will not eat you. Better you be carrion for the eaterworms."

"So," said the Meatbringer. "More of your great wit." He bowed. "This meat I carry hampers me. May I cut it loose?"

"Certainly," said Annelyn.

"Let me place it inside, out of the way," the Meatbringer said. "So we might not trip over it."

Annelyn nodded, and circled warily to the side, suppressing a smile. He knew what the Meatbringer intended. The other took his knife and slit the knots that bound the child to his back, then placed the body on the far side of the door. He turned, framed by the purplish light.

Laughing, he said, "The *yaga-la-hai* and the grouns, you are so alike. Animals." He reached out and swung shut the wide doors, and again Annelyn's ears rang to the clang he had heard once, long ago.

"No," Annelyn said. "Alike, yes. But not animals." He put on his helmet. The thick darkness vanished like a mist.

The Meatbringer had danced silently and deftly to one side. A great grin split his face, and he advanced with stealthy steps, his knife ready to thrust and disembowel.

If Annelyn — like the late, unfortunate Groff — had tried a rush attack on the place where the Meatbringer had *been*, in the last instant of light, the thrust would have left him open and vulnerable to a fatal stab from the Meatbringer where he now *was*. It was a crafty, polished technique; but Annelyn could see. For once, darkness and deception were of no use. And Annelyn's rapier was longer than the Meatbringer's knife.

Quickly, easily, casually, Annelyn turned to face his enemy, smiled beneath his helmet, and lunged. The Meatbringer hardly had time to react; it had been years since he had fought on even terms. Annelyn ran him through the abdomen.

Afterward, he pushed the body down the air shaft, and prayed that it would fall eternally.

The Masque of the Manworm was still in progress in the High Burrow when Annelyn returned to the *yaga-la-hai.* In the dusty libraries, men in dominoes and women in veils writhed and spun; the treasure rooms were open for viewing, the pleasure chambers open for other things; in the Highest Hall, the Second Vermentor lay beneath a thousand torches while the worm-children danced past him, and sang chants of his demise. The Manworm had no face now; he was one with the White Worm. Beside him, the priest-surgeons stood, in white smocks with scalpel-and-theta, as they had stood for a week. The Seventh Feast had just been laid.

Caralee was there, bright golden Caralee, and the bronze knights, and many who had once been friends of Annelyn. But most only smiled and made soft witticisms when he came striding unexpectedly through the doors.

Some, perhaps, did not recognize him. Only a short time ago, at the Sun Masque, he had been brilliant in silk and spidergray. Now he was painfully gaunt, cut and bruised in a dozen places, his eyes restless in dark hollows, and the only clothes he wore were black tatters that hung on him like a mushroom farmer's foul rags. His face was bare, without so much as a domino, and that set the guests to muttering, since the time of unmasking had not yet come.

Very soon they had more to mutter about. For Annelyn, this strange, changling Annelyn, stood silently in the door, his eyes jumping from one mask to another. Then, still silent, he walked across the gleaming obsidian floor to the feasting table, seized an iron platter piled high with fine white groun-flesh, and flung it violently across the room. A few laughed; others, not so amused, picked slices of meat from their shoulders. Annelyn went from the room.

Afterward, he became a familiar figure among the *yaga-la-hai*, though he lost his flair for dress and much of his fine wit. Instead, he spoke endlessly and persuasively of forgotten crimes and the sins of bygone eons, painting deliciously dark pictures of monster worms who bred beneath the House and would one day rise to consume all. He was fond of telling the worm-children that they ought to lie with grouns, instead of cooking them, so that a new people might be fashioned to resist his nightmare worms.

In the endless long decay of the House of the Worm, nothing was so prized as novelty. Annelyn, though considered coarse and most unsubtle, wove entertaining tales and had a spark of shocking irreverence. Thus, though the bronze knights grumbled, he was allowed to live.

Behavioral scientists have greatly extended our understanding of human psychology individually and in the mass, through studies of people in controlled environments and situations. But there's a dark side of the human psyche that sometimes emerges when it's least expected. Here Gene Wolfe writes of a behavioral program that produced chilling effects.

Gene Wolfe won the Nebula Award of the Science Fiction Writers of America in 1974 for his novella *The Death of Dr. Island*, a story based on psychological experimentation. Here he turns to a related theme, in a story whose title seems less and less playful as the narrative progresses.

When I Was Ming the Merciless

Gene Wolfe

"Thank you. Is it permissible for me to sit? Fine. No, I cannot complain, really. . . .

"I'd like to say that everyone here has been as courteous as could be expected — that isn't quite true, actually, but you know what I mean. No one has struck me.

"No, I don't smoke. I'd appreciate some coffee, though. That was one of the things we missed — coffee. At least at first. There was a lot of tea in the supplies, but no coffee. I used to enjoy it while I was in there — tea, I mean — but now I can't tolerate the taste.

"I don't know if it was intentional or not. I thought you would know.

"It's odd that you should put it as you did. Because I've thought of it so often myself, since the end, in just that way. I remember how things used to be . . . the way I used to be myself, outside. And the next thing I think of is the psych-aids breaking through the wall with the butts of their guns, and the way my guards fought them. We had polearms, you know. Polearms and swords — the swords were reserved for officers. Somebody told me a few days ago that three of the psych-aids were hurt; but I feel sure it must have been more than that. We were surprised, of course — anyone would have been under the circumstances. Still, we fought well. My guards were well trained, and every one of them, man or woman, was a warrior of proven bravery.

"Listen, you don't have to stop him like that. That was a legitimate question, 'Aren't you ashamed?' And I'll give him a legitimate answer — no, I am not ashamed. I am proud of the Empire, proud of what we did, proud of the way we fought at the end. It was a fight we couldn't win, but we fought well. That's what matters — fighting well. Who wins is a matter of chance and advantage.

"You don't have to tell me to relax; I am perfectly relaxed. I raised my voice only to bring home my point to you — it's a little trick I have, just like pounding the arm of the chair as I pronounce each word.

"We were talking about morality, and I feel that is a more

fruitful and interesting subject; but I can tell you very briefly how we constructed our weapons, if you want — provided you understand that we are going to return to the moral question afterward.

"No, I feel no need whatsoever to justify myself — not to you or to anyone else. But I want to make you understand the imperatives of the situation. After all, that was the whole point of the experiment: to clarify the imperatives of that type of situation. What was the use of all that time. . . .

"Oh Jesus, the building and the fighting. . . .

"I'm sorry. I'm all right. Thank you for the coffee. The polearms were easy, really. There were several cleavers in the kitchen, and a lot of knives. We sawed the handles off brooms and mops, and joined two of them together. We made scarf joints at the ends — do you know what a scarf is? Like a step in the wood, to give the glue more area. There was a glue in the wood shop that was stronger than the wood itself, if you let it set up overnight. We made tests, you see. Glued up pieces and broke them afterward. We made saw-cuts in the ends of the poles, and put the knife blades into them, clamped them, and glued them in place. Afterward we put nails through the holes in the tangs — that was just extra insurance. Out here there will be more scope for ingenuity; we might even be able to get hold of some fissionables. Just joking, of course.

"In there, the cleavers were the best of the kitchen material. We put them about twenty centimeters down the shaft, then put a boning-knife blade in the end. With a weapon like that, the warrior could hack or stab; it was almost as good as a sword.

"The swords were the most difficult to make — that was why I restricted them, made them only for officers. Then too, in that way they served as badges of rank. We tore up the floors in the Graphic Arts Center to get the steel reinforcing bars, and heated them in the furnace burner, then pounded them out. A lot of them broke, and had to be reforged — sometimes over and over. I had the best one, naturally. I suppose you people have it now?

"Yes, I suppose I *would* like to see it — I carried it in some good fights. You wouldn't understand about that. The hilt was bone, almost like ivory, and I had Althea burn the Lung-Rin into the bone. Althea was our best artist.

"The Lung-Rin? That is the symbol of the Empire — two dragons fighting.

"No, we didn't worship the Lung-Rin. It was a symbol, that's all. In the long run, if you know what I mean, *we* were the Lung-Rin. We had ceremonies, yes. We set up a figure to represent all the Yellows. Don made it of wood and leather, and that was the center of the ceremonies. Althea helped him with the face, and I had her make it look something like me — you understand, a little psychology. It's odd, but you can make a thing like that, and have everyone bow in front of it, and offer it the things we took in war, and after a time it becomes . . . I don't know, something more. More than just the figure you set up in the beginning. Have you talked to Don?

"He had a theory — I don't know whether he believed it himself. I didn't, but still. . . . There was something in it. Do you understand what I mean? It wasn't true; but still. . . .

"All right, here's what he thought. Or anyway, what he

said he thought. That there are things we don't know about that live in the world with us — things in another plane of reality. And when you make something like that, it comes — one of them comes. It shapes itself to fit your image of it, becoming the real Spirit of the Yellows. Anyway, when we had the torchlight processions, sometimes you might think you could see it move. It was just the flickering light, of course, and the fact that because it was so tall the face was illuminated from the bottom. Any face will look strange when you light it from below, I suppose. We caught rats and pigeons when we built it and put them inside, so it would make strange sounds; some of them must have lived a long time.

"No, I don't know what happened to it, and I don't care. You can't kill the *thing*, the Spirit of the Yellows. Not unless you kill all of us, and you won't do that. We'll be free someday. How could we forget? The experiment was the greatest thing in our lives. At night, before we had won, we used to sit around the fire — outside, the buildings were too dangerous then — and talk. You've never done that. You weren't there.

"No, not about what we were going to do when we won — at least, not mostly. Not even about our plans for the next day. Mostly we talked about our lives before the experiment. Each of us would tell the rotten things that had happened to him, and then someone else would talk. We never said it, but we were all thinking that it wasn't like that here. We were all together — all Yellows together. That was one of the first things we did, I think about the fourth day after the gates closed. We swore that we were going to stand together or fall together; there wasn't going to be any splitting. We had seen what happened to the Greens; they were always going in all directions; they wouldn't support each other. By the time they got organized it was too late. The others had the weapons and the organization and the fighting spirit. They'd been knocked down too much, and they'd been cut up too much — do you understand what I mean? If you take people like that, and beat them over and over and over again, most of them stay beaten. One or two will go the other way — become so hard and strong that they're as good as anything you've got. But not most of them. So when the one or two try and lead them, there's no support. Then too, there's the sexual effect. Maybe I shouldn't talk about this. Do you want to turn off the recorder?

"Well, all right. Everybody saw, almost from the beginning, that the women would have to fight just like the men. Jan was the best woman warrior we had, and she came out for it from the beginning. The Blues were already doing it, and if we didn't, we'd lose. Besides, if the women didn't fight, there couldn't be real equality, because if a woman said we ought to stand up to the other colors, all the men would say it wasn't her that was going to bleed.

"Some of the women didn't want to, of course. And some of the men didn't want to have them do it, either. I'd say that there were perhaps eight women against, and five men. That was where the drill came in. Most of all, there. It's hard — very hard to get people to drill. You've got to work it in a little bit at a time. But once they do it, they learn to obey orders, and when you say, 'Come on!' they follow. I started them with practice in using weapons (it was just the knives and clubs then) and formalized it later. I said even if they weren't going to fight, the least they could do was practice with the rest of us; and then if they had to sometime, they'd know how. Of course after we were better organized I could have simply ordered it; but I didn't have that kind of authority then — I wasn't Emperor.

"No, I was a political science major. A lot were psych students, and a lot more were from the school of sociology. I never noticed that they behaved differently than the rest of us.

"What I was coming to, was that when a man — a male, let's call him — has been fighting a woman, and he wins and knocks her down, and she drops whatever it is she has, a club or whatever, and perhaps she's bleeding where he cut her or broke her lip, and often her shirt and shorts are torn, there is an impulse that takes command. Perhaps women don't feel that way, but men do. And then, when a woman has had that happen once or twice, it takes everything out of them. They won't fight anymore; they just want to run, or sometimes to hide. Some of the men said that they really liked it, underneath, but I don't think so. Still, they were the ones, mostly, who wanted to join us.

"No, of course we didn't let them. We couldn't let them. That was the point of the whole thing. We had the bands — I've still got mine, see, around my wrist — and we couldn't get them off. You can't get them off. Once they clamped your bracelet on you, you were a Yellow or a Blue or a Green; and that was it. Some of the Greens, particularly, tried to cut them off before we got control of all the tools. It couldn't be done; a file won't even scratch them.

"Did that bother you? The clothes? Yes, we had colored clothes to begin with — yellow shorts and shirts. But they didn't really matter; it was the wristbands. In the end I had all my guards go naked to the waist, with just a strip of yellow cloth around their heads to identify them. You see, I had noticed that the braver someone was, the more torn up their shirts got, until the best of them really didn't have any at all.

"Yes, the women too. I'll tell you a secret. When you go out to fight, anything you can do that will make you look different — strange — helps. It takes the heart out of the others. I think the Blues had the advantage at first — those dark blue shirts and shorts. They looked like Federal Police. But the naked chests and the yellow head-rags took care of that. We kept together and came at them in a solid mass — swords in front, and the polearms poking between them, and everybody yelling. That's very important. And the flag. I gave my own shirt to make the flag. The front was all cut up by then, but there wasn't a rip in the back — not one. That was the part we took off and used for the flag. Althea sewed the Lung-Rin in it with red thread. Some of them said it would never stand out because there wasn't enough air movement in the building, where most of the fighting was. I told them that if they went forward fast enough it would stand out, and I was right. It was useful in another way too: once or twice we were scattered — I remember one time when the Blues ambushed us — and it showed us where our center was. Nils carried it. I don't know what's happened to it now. It would be nice to have when we get back together.

"I've already told you about that. It couldn't be done: if

you were a Yellow, you were a Yellow; a Blue was a Blue, and a Green was a Green; and nothing anybody could say made any difference. Jan had a Green slave-lover for a while — he even fought with us a couple of times against the Blues. The Greens were finished by then, and he wasn't much good.

"No, as I said, the Greens had a few real fighters. I have no idea what their names were. That was one of the first rules I made — Greens and Blues have no names. If you knew one of them by name before the experiment, you forgot it as quickly as possible. If we had to talk about one particularly, we said: 'the blond Blue woman,' or 'Jan's Green boy.' Like that.

"Another thing that helped us fight was the idea of the Empire. If you talk about a thing like that, it becomes real. Just like the figure we set up. We had the Imperial Guards, and they were brave because if they weren't, they'd lose their places, they wouldn't be guards anymore; and the others fought harder hoping to get in — if someone distinguished himself, or herself, I made them a guard. And if a guard did, I made that guard an officer. And once I had the guards, I used them to keep the rest in order.

"What it was about? The whole experiment? You know — the world. Only so many resources, you see, and so *many* groups of people. I understand some of the other runnings of the experiment came out a little differently; but they wanted to see how *we* worked it out — what our solution was. That's why I don't feel bad about what we did. It was our problem, set to us (if you want to put it that way), and we solved it. When they broke the wall we were organized —

everyone knew his place, who he took orders from, and how much he got. How much food, drinking water, bathwater. That was the Empire.

"Mostly we just called it that: 'The Empire.' Officially, we began by calling it Mongolia. Because we were the Yellows. Later we shortened it.

"No, I don't feel bad about her, whoever she was. We were all volunteers, originally, you have to remember. And she kept getting out of line, over and over again, when she was just a stinking Green or Blue or whatever she was. I can't even remember. So I decided she should be punished. We made a ceremony out of it, with fire in the braziers, and the big gong.

"I had Jan do it. Jan was a colonel. Neal and Ted held her, and Jan put the sword through her belly — so she'd live long enough to know what was happening. When Jan pulled it out, she licked the blood from the blade. The rest of the Greens and Blues would have obeyed after that, believe me.

"Yes, when she finally died. That was when they broke down the wall. They were monitoring a few selected individuals, I suppose, though we didn't know it. She must have been one of them.

"Naturally. I understand how you feel about it now — how the school feels and how the public and the President feel. But do you understand how we felt? You haven't been through what we went through together. We have learned a great many things we will remember, but none of you could possibly know how it was then, when I was Ming the Merciless."

We're just beginning to realize that humans can possess more sensory abilities than the traditional five: sight, hearing, touch, smell, and taste. Some of us can evidently read minds, perceive colors by touch, detect underground stores of water. And when you consider the evolutionary theory of compensation, which says that individuals who lack one survival mechanism can stay alive if they're gifted with an "extra" one, you may wonder if a blind woman, for instance, might have some extra talents — she might be a telepath, or even a chronopath, able to see into the minds of creatures that lived hundreds of millions of years ago.

But would that help her to survive in the increasingly dangerous inner cities of tomorrow?

Steven Utley is a young writer from Texas who has produced an impressive number of outstanding stories in the past few years; *Predators* is sure to add to his growing reputation.

Predators

Steven Utley

"CAN YOU TELL ME where you are, Vivian?" asked Dr. Mayes, three feet and two million years away from her.

"Africa, perhaps. It looks like Africa, anyway. It's hot and bright. Late morning or early afternoon. The savanna seems to stretch at least five hundred kilometers in every direction. I can see the barest outline of mountains to the . . . I don't know yet, no directional orientation's possible at the moment. My host is moving through deep brown grass. There doesn't seem to be much large animal life close at hand. A few birds that are too far away for me to identify positively, though they may be condors of some kind. And something else that looks like a species of mastodon. It's feeding about two hundred meters to our left. . . ."

The minutest details of the Pliocene landscape flowed out of Vivian's skull, were sucked out of her mind by the dime-sized metal disks taped to her temples and forehead, were sent running along fine wires of copper, were fed into circuit-crammed plastic boxes that digested the information and transferred it onto spooled tape. The room was filled with the hushed, liquid murmurings of recording and interpreting devices. Regina whimpered in her sleep. Vivian droned on softly.

". . . My host is hungry and on the move. The mastodon's seen us and calls out a warning, but we ignore it. The beast is too big to tackle. We have another scent now, and my host is getting excited. There's some sort of large herd just barely visible in the distance, it must be a kilometer or two away, but there's a strong, warm wind moving across the savanna, so the air's full of dust and scent. I get a mental impression of some kind of gnulike creature. We're moving in on the herd with impatient slowness, saving strength for the kill."

Vivian leaned slightly forward in her seat, fascinated by the tensing and relaxing of hard, stringy muscle as her host, the hunter, homed in on the prey scent. Dragonflies whirled away at the hunting beast's approach. Grasshoppers seemed to explode from the very ground ahead, alarmed by the fall of massive, padded paws. An odd golden bird screeched defiantly, banking low overhead. Vivian's host sneezed violently as a gnat buzzed up its nose.

The hunter seemed tireless. It quickened its pace slightly, falling into a trot, and did not slow to a walk until the herd lay close, covering the savanna. The herbivores were brown, shiny-flanked beasts. Ungainly youngsters played under the watchful eyes of formidable-looking adults. The hunter flattened itself against the earth and surveyed the prospects.

A bull snorted and pawed the dirt, unable to see or hear or smell the flesh-eater, but evidently aware of a sudden wrongness in the air. The mood was infectious: other bulls began to bellow and stamp. The cows shifted and milled nervously. The youngsters froze in place.

The hunting beast was among them too quickly for them to organize their defense. The charge resulted in a rout—the adults reared, wheeled, ran, and the young beasts had no choice but to be carried along with their elders.

The hunting beast lunged among them, head down, ears back, eyes intent upon one whose confusion had lasted a second too long. The calf started, spun, bleated as the shadow of its killer filled the air. A split second before the moment of impact, Vivian caught a glimpse of the victim's large, round, incredibly moist eye, and then the hunter had its prey by the neck vertebrae. The long canines went through skin, muscle, and bone, like pruning shears snapping through small branches. Blood spurted into the air.

The carnivore gave its prey a shake and let go. The calf twitched and lay still. The hunter sat back, a golden shape in the center of a settling cloud of dust, and contemplated first the nearly decapitated animal under its forepaws and then the retreating mass of the spooked herd. Two golden birds dipped past, surveying the tableau of victor and victim. *Vivian*, one of the birds seemed to say.

Vivian gasped.

"Vivian, are you all right?"

She listened to the hunting beast's heavy breathing for a moment, then said, almost tentatively, "Yes." The carnivore sniffed its dinner and cracked its jaws in a dagger-toothed grin of triumph. "Yes. I . . . oh shit, I'm —"

"What is it? What's wrong?"

She shushed the voice and gnawed the inside of her cheek. The Pliocene sky was lightening. The grays, greens, and browns of the savanna were fading. The dark hide of the slain calf suddenly had a bleached cast to it.

"I'm losing it!"

"Try to maintain contact, Vivian."

"I *am* trying, but it's fading, I'm losing it, it's going. God damn it."

All around Vivian, the recording and interpreting instruments continued to gurgle softly, but the Pliocene period had slipped away from her. She sighed and settled back into leather upholstery, eyes closed, skin tingling at the touch of the metal receptors attached to her face. She jerked when a finger brushed her forehead lightly.

"Are you all right?" asked Dr. Mayes, gently smoothing down the corner of a patch of white tape on her skin.

"Just disgusted, that's all. I'm sorry the morning's been such an abort. I don't seem to have any control today."

"It's nothing to worry about," the doctor said soothingly. "Relax. We all have our off days."

"It's not my time of the month, if that's what you mean."

"Vivian!"

Vivian laughed, then gestured for the doctor's hand. He gave it to her. "Dr. Mayes," she said, "you're such a prude."

"Show some respect for my gray hairs, young lady."

"Hmm. Would it be impertinent of me to ask how old you are? Or should I just give you a quick, painless jab to the forebrain and find out for myself?"

She heard him laugh softly. "As if it were any of your business, I'm sixty-seven years old."

"I was only seven years off on my guess. Well. Would you like me to try establishing contact again?"

The doctor withdrew his hand from hers and said, "No, I don't think so. The morning's just about used up, and Colin has his own project to set up. He'll need the room this afternoon. I suggest that you rest and get your nerves straightened out."

"Nerves?" Vivian frowned, eyes still closed. She felt herself tremble as she thought of a Pliocene animal's wet, round eye.

Dr. Mayes began to carefully peel off the tape. "I know you had some trouble on your way here this morning. Regina had somebody's blood all over her when you came in. So Dr. Simons told me."

"Yes," muttered Vivian, very tense now. "Yes. He cleaned her up for me."

"I know. Vivian, I'm going to talk to Le Sage after I get

you out of this rig. I'm pretty certain that she'll approve what I have to suggest. After all, you're the most adept chronopath we have, and you've got all of those latent abilities we're only now finding out about. Almost an entire catalog of psi talents. You're a scientific bonanza, Vivian, much too valuable to lose. We don't want anything bad happening to you."

Vivian drew her head away from his hands for a moment. "What is it you have to suggest?"

"I want you to think about coming here to live."

"Here?" Vivian smiled. "Why, that sounds almost like a proposition, Doctor. Almost, but not quite."

"Don't be facetious, young lady. I'm serious. You could move into a room of your own here at the Institute, and you wouldn't have to worry about any unpleasantnesses like the one this morning."

"How will I get my daily constitutional if I don't walk to and from work?"

"For God's sake, this isn't a joking matter. You could have been killed today. You would have been, had it not been for Regina. You're not safe on the streets."

Vivian felt the smile die on her face. "No one is safe on the streets. I take the same chances everyone else does."

"No! You're at a considerable disadvantage —"

"Regina makes up for that!" Vivian snapped, abruptly angry. She felt the last of the tape come away from her skin and knew that she was once again severed from the instruments, severed from the computer on the floor below. Severed from her eyes. She did not move from her seat.

"Regina talkes care of me," she went on, forcing herself to speak calmly. "That's her job, that's what I have her for."

"Regina isn't invincible," the doctor countered. "Vivian, I *worry* about you whenever you're not here at the Institute. You don't know what it's like outside. You've never really seen your own day and age except through other people's eyes."

"I can hear and smell it by myself. I can even taste it."

"Vivian —"

"I actually do taste it, Dr. Mayes. The air, I mean. I know how it changes from day to day. I'm becoming quite an authority on the different flavors of dirt in the air."

"That's part of what I'm talking about! The world is falling apart outside. There's crap everywhere. And people are going insane in the streets. They'll just as soon kill you as look at you. This morning, for instance. Do you really know what happened? Do you know *why* Regina had to tear up whoever it was that threatened you?"

"I, uh, I was too surprised to find out at the time," she admitted. "I might still be able to find out from Regina."

"No, let me speculate first," the doctor continued. "It wasn't for money. You don't carry any. You don't even carry a purse. So let's see. Rape, perhaps? No, I still don't think so. Rapists are a very strange lot, Vivian, they don't really seem to care what their victims look like, just as long as the victims are female. But, even so — and I trust you'll pardon my saying so — you are not one to arouse anything like uncontrollable primal lust in the male breast."

"I know pretty much what I look like," Vivian replied evenly.

"So. We'll rule out rape. No, I think that whatever happened, happened simply because you arrived at a given point at a given moment, and a given person was there. And he or she, whichever, simply felt like killing whoever was available. And, Vivian, this goes on every day, every hour. There are murderers and potential murderers everywhere. Think about it. The odds are overwhelmingly against you. You're blind. You have Regina, but you also have a world that's become so rotten that a steadily increasing number of essentially decent but understandably desperate people are turning into psychopathic killers. Killing is the only thrill left. No. It's more than a thrill. It's the only luxury left, because the only thing we now have more than enough of is people. You are not safe outside. You in particular. A blind woman and a big dog are no match for a city full of homicidal maniacs."

Vivian put her face into her hands and concentrated on Regina, who still slept fitfully on the floor beside Vivian's chair. Regina dreamed murkily, in gray-shaded flashes, and dipping through that unhuman fog was not easy. Vivian's telepathic talents were considerably less refined than her chronopathic abilities, but she was delicate enough in her probing of the dog's memories. The cautiously extracted memory to which she attached herself was a fuzzy, canine-perspective replay of the morning's incident: the opaque-eyed stranger's menacing approach, Regina's warning growl, a quick, over-the-shoulder glance to make certain that

Vivian knew that something was amiss and that she was to be perfectly still. Then the stranger's lunge, the knife, the dog's dodge and counterattack, blood, the taste and smell of blood, the stranger's mangled hand waving about frantically, slinging blood, howls, peripheral glimpses of other strangers stepping out into the street and hurrying past in order to avoid becoming embroiled in the melee, shrieks of agony from the stranger thrashing on the sidewalk, slinging blood, clawing and kicking, gurgling. Regina watched the other strangers hurrying past, lapping up the blood with their eyes as they passed, but passing quickly, staying well away from the enormous dog and the rigidly motionless woman, pointedly refusing to join in a fellow human being's lost battle against so implacable a guardian angel. . . .

Vivian came away from Regina and sat up, shivering violently. She reached for the doctor's hand again, and again he let her have it.

"Did you . . . ?" Dr. Mayes's question trailed off.

Vivian nodded. "I . . . I appreciate your concern for me," she said slowly. "I really do. But I'm comfortable in my apartment. I know my way around there. I don't mind living alone. I'm used to it."

Dr. Mayes sighed loudly, obviously exasperated. "I wish I could order you to stay here. For your own sake. For the sake of psi research. Hell, for the sake of my own peace of mind, if nothing else."

Vivian kissed his hand and let it go, then smiled. "I suppose I should be grateful for *that* much, at least."

"What?"

"Oh, well, even if I'm not one to arouse primal lust in the male breast, I certainly seem to have stoked up your paternal fires. Don't you have any children of your own?"

"Don't mock me, Vivian," he quietly replied.

"I'm sorry. Hmpf. I love you, Dr. Mayes. Even though you are sixty-seven years old. Even though you are absolutely the biggest worrywart I've ever known."

"Please think about what I've said. The world outside is no place for a —"

"Blind, twenty-five-year-old virgin with no tits and a fat ass."

"For heaven's sake!" The doctor sounded sincerely shocked.

"You said it first," Vivian mildly reminded him. "Or implied as much, at any rate." She stood up and smoothed the front of her dress. Regina rose at her side and thrust a cold, moist nose into her hand. She gave the dog an affectionate pat on the jowl. "So we'll call it a day," she said to the doctor. "Same time tomorrow?"

"Yes. Try not to let what happened this morning upset you. Get some sleep. I want you in good shape tomorrow. And, uh, as I said, please think about it, about living here at the Institute."

"You do persist," Vivian said as he helped her into her coat. "But I'm perfectly adjusted to the outside world. It's really not so bad in the street, Doctor. It's actually quite interesting. You've been cooped up here for too long. You should get out more often."

"Be careful, Vivian."

"Oh, don't fret so. Come on, Regina, we have a city full of killers to lick."

"*Vivian.*"

"Ta, Doctor."

With her hand on Regina's harness, Vivian let herself be led out of the building. Woman and dog were a long-familiar sight to the guards at the door. They did not ask to see her identification card, only mumbled vague farewells as she passed. Vivian murmured something in reply and then, because the day was still very cold, paused on the steps outside to acclimate herself. Regina nuzzled her thigh questioningly.

Vivian sniffed the air, made a face, and listened to the sounds of closely packed humanity on the street before her. She picked up mental gibberish, onion-layered thoughts received from many people simultaneously, and sorted through it interestedly. Nothing new, she decided. The same old despair, the fear, the hatred, the sense of oppression, the screaming need to lash out at whatever, whoever, was there to be lashed out at. A little stronger today, a little deeper, growing all the time, growing by the hour. "Critical mass encroacheth," she muttered to the uncomprehending dog. "Okay. Let's go, Regina."

She let herself be half led, half dragged homeward by Regina while she reviewed her conversation with Dr. Mayes. And then there was the Pliocene trip, and the details of the morning's incident, the sight, smell, and taste of blood, the sound of her would-have-been attacker's shrieks, the feel of his flesh and bone between Regina's teeth, the glimpse of the doomed calf's eye, vertebrae snapping in jaws more dreadful than Regina's, golden, screeching birds overhead and the stranger gurgling on the ground, the images superimposing themselves over one another in a mad rush. Vivian, shuddering at the memories, paused, bent low to stroke Regina's fur, and whispered into the dog's ear, "Sweet work, girl."

And Vivian laughed to herself and opened her thoughts to a city full of homicidal maniacs and called out gleefully from behind her blind eyes, *Here I am, here I am, come and get me. If you can.*

We turn now to other worlds, and a story of unexpected menace on a planet whose native vegetation gives off a gas that induces greater concentration in the mental processes of those who breathe it. But some human mental processes can become dangerous when they're intensified. . . .

Cherry Wilder was born in New Zealand and lives in West Germany. She has written poetry, plays, and short stories for markets ranging from men's magazines to literary quarterlies, but only recently has she turned to science fiction; two of her stories have been published in England, and *The Remittance Man* marks her debut on the U.S. science fiction scene.

The Remittance Man

Cherry Wilder

THEY FLEW OVER the polar ice cap two minutes ahead of the rising Star.

"Watch this!" said Dietrich.

A wave of light broke over the top of the world, blue-white at first, then as the light reached the helicopter the land below them flared into irregular patches of bright gold.

Lieutenant Harris gave an eager gasp; the camera churred into action.

"What causes that?" asked Captain Blake.

"Lichen," said Dietrich. "We're over the tundra. There are the lakes. Big one we call Lake Fish; the string of smaller ones have . . . er . . . female names. Anna, Buttercup, Clover, Daisy and Elsa."

"The whole herd," said Captain Blake.

"You're right, Captain!" he grinned. "From up here you can see the first small lake has the shape of a cow's udder. Some of us are country boys."

The lieutenant laughed. The young M.O. looked at his two passengers, still grinning broadly.

"Did I miss something?" he asked.

"My name is Elsa," said the captain easily.

Dietrich blushed. He tried to catch the lieutenant's eye but she was bent over the camera.

"I was named for a lioness," said the captain. "What's your first name, Dr. Dietrich?"

"Walter," he said. "Lieutenant? Care to check in?"

"My first name is Tracey." She gave poor Dietrich, at last, a cold, insolent stare. "Can we get lower in this craft, Doctor?"

He reduced altitude too fast. They hovered a hundred meters above the smooth, gray waters of Lake Clover. Elsa Blake could see the colonies of lichen on the rocks by the shore and beyond them the thick crumpled growth of land-kelp. Every shade of green but no trees, no tree trunks.

"Where are those 'high pines' the commander promised us?" she asked.

"Coming up!" said Dietrich.

"Do they work?" asked Tracey Harris.

"Who knows?" He laughed. "They contain this stimulant . . . vegetable oil, a little like turpentine. Guys working among them say it's refreshing . . . aids concentration . . . you know. . . ."

"Sounds like a plug for chewing gum," said Harris. Dietrich wilted again.

Elsa Blake looked down at the sargasso sea of kelp and algae; the temperature outside was minus five degrees Celsius, a summer day. Inside she had to watch this sadistic mating game Harris played with the young guys on isolated stations. The cold shoulder. Impossible to explore the tundra on foot . . . maybe the damned kelp bit you. There were those planks down in Ose National Park, wonderfully green there too, with iris and water lilies and the students hiking over the boards. . . .

The Captain sighed and said, "Did the ice come down this far?"

"Right down." The doctor nodded. "The lake chain is depressed: the path of an old glacier. This last winter the glacier reestablished and came down pretty near to Elsa . . . the last lake, I mean."

They flew over a field of strewn boulders and came, without warning, to a huge rift valley filled with debris from the recent thaw.

"An animal!" exclaimed Tracey Harris. "I saw a dead animal!"

"One of the mintos," said Dietrich. "Large grazing rodent. Like a capybara. We might see a herd of them."

"A rodent? A rat the size of a sheep?"

"They grow nearly that size," agreed Dietrich. "Didn't you see the rugs Savage made from minto hides?"

"Oh yeah," said Tracey. "He promised to show me a checkered one he keeps in his room."

Walter Dietrich swallowed hard and began a dissertation on the climate. The captain looked down thankfully at long slopes covered with something very like pine trees.

"Is that an outstation?" she asked suddenly.

Dietrich's glance at his instruments showed that he had drifted a point or so off course.

"More or less," he said. "We call it the Lodge." The building among the high pines was a rambling structure of stone and metal.

"Great!" said the lieutenant. "We can stretch our legs."

"The place is off limits," said Dietrich uneasily. "Didn't the C.O. mention . . . ?"

"Not a word," said Captain Blake. She looked down, wondering; there was no landing pad but a wide clearing among the trees. A tendril of smoke rose above the pine tops.

"Doctor," she demanded, "is the Lodge occupied?"

"Yes," admitted Dietrich, "there is one guy down there."

"Let's visit," said the lieutenant. "Come on, Walter, baby."

"Hell . . ." said Dietrich. "We can't just go there. Kaldor is not a member of the base complement. He's some kind of recluse."

"Kaldor?"

Elsa Blake gave a shuddering laugh. She stared down at the humped roofs of the Lodge, and continued looking down because the shock had made her eyes fill with tears. Kaldor. It was the same man, of course. Small universe. How self-absorbed, how settled, how mad he must have become. He used to drink Tokay and sit on the porch with Mick, yarning about the birth of continents. He sent a wire when she finished her training: "Pity. Your goulash was so good." He went tirelessly in support of his theories to remote places on the earth. On one furlough she found him on the porch again, withdrawn and scraggy after a bad spell in Antarctica. Years and light-years in between, and now here was the impossible coincidence.

"Franz Kaldor . . . the glaciologist?"

"That's his name," said Dietrich.

"Then we must land," said Elsa. "I'll clear it with Commander Gregg. Kaldor is an old friend."

Dietrich protested, but Elsa pulled rank and slapped him down. Lieutenant Harris exchanged a warmer glance with Dietrich that said "Old Dragon"; she moistened her lips.

"You could always say we ran out of gas . . . Walter."

Dietrich brightened up and circled lower.

"Wait!" said the captain. "How much contact does Kaldor have with the base?"

"We pass on his supplies from Procne," said Dietrich. "Seems he has big research backing at home. Years ago . . . eight . . . the base crew helped dig his foundations."

"What work is he doing?"

"Ice," said Dietrich. "Arctic flora. In summer we see him out on the moraine, as far north as Mount Byrd."

"Can we radio the Lodge?" asked Elsa.

"Ma'am, I doubt if he'll answer," Dietrich said earnestly. "He shuns contact, unless there's trouble. . . ."

"Trouble?"

Dietrich had the air of a man treading on thin ice.

"I guess you heard about the copter crash last year. Kaldor brought in the survivor . . . Ensign Ball."

"Are there many emergencies?"

"The thing is, Captain, that Itys *looks* hospitable," he explained.

"Good atmosphere," agreed Elsa. "Small land mass."

"A great place to hibernate," said the lieutenant.

"Survey parties — we call 'em tourists — come in from the colonies on Procne. We even had expeditions from Philomel." The doctor warmed to his subject. "They come rugged up for winter sports and get lost in a blizzard. Kaldor has made other rescues."

"He sounds like a regular Saint Bernard." Tracey shivered. "Let's check out his brandy."

They descended from light into the dry shade of the pines. Dietrich cut the rotors and they sat in silence staring at the low, cavernous porch of Kaldor's house. The Lodge stared back: the window slits were eye sockets, the porch roof was a beetling brow. Elsa Blake was more doubtful now, about the method of her approach at least. She must attempt to make contact — the language of the manual came easily — but there was no reason to expose the two kids to any awkward situation.

Just then the metal door swung open like a dark mouth and Kaldor stepped out.

At fifty meters he was quite unchanged; a solid, dark man,

neatly proportioned, with a distinctive roundness to his head. In loose trousers and a parka he looked like an Eskimo.

"Let me speak to him," said Elsa. She opened her door, and hit on another snippet of alien approach procedure. "We'll all get out and I'll make contact."

The M.O. reached automatically for his canteen and medical kit; she was glad to see that he was unarmed.

Kaldor stood patiently with his gloved hands clasped in front of him. He did not stir until she was three meters away, and then he jutted his head out in a characteristic manner.

"Franz . . . ?"

"Who . . . ?"

His smile flickered uncertainly. He shifted his boots and shaded his eyes in a parody of shyness. The voice was creaking and rusty with disuse.

"I'm Elsa. Do you remember?"

"*Elsa!*"

It was heartfelt; good enough for her. She strode up to him and they embraced, ritually. Kaldor had an acrid gamy stink; his parka was of minto hide.

"You are the same!" he said. "Elsa! This is fine!"

"Franz . . . let me look at you."

She steadied him, one step above her on the porch, which brought their heads level. She knew more or less how she had changed in fifteen years but the change in Kaldor was harder to assess. He was high-colored; his limp black hair was plastered down on his skull and worked into a long pigtail. His face, under a grizzled beard, was gaunt; his eyes were bloodshot and restless. Not right yet. She wondered about endemic diseases, fever, even tuberculosis. She restrained an impulse to strip off her glove and lay a hand on his forehead.

"Kaldor . . . what are you doing here . . . on Itys . . . all alone?"

He chuckled and blinked. "Out of sight." He spoke in rapid bursts. "Packed off, almost. Dealing with the ice — with survival. They know I'm here, eh? I want for nothing."

"Franz, I must tell you. Mick has gone."

"You mean . . . ?"

She nodded; it was no longer painful to speak of it. "He died five years ago. Heart attack."

Kaldor clucked with his tongue. "He was a good friend. And your boy?"

"Andy is fine. Still on the Kenyan reserve with his family."

"You have grandchildren?"

She grinned. "Half a dozen . . . all beautiful. It's a commune."

For a moment she longed for Mick; she could see him and Kaldor talking on the white, sunlit porch in Florida, years ago. Kaldor was scraggy and sick, as if he were still recuperating from Antarctica.

"What have you brought me?" he asked. "Lovebirds?"

The lieutenant and the M.O. were wandering up, arm in arm, through the high pines. Kaldor shook hands obediently, sizing up the newcomers. He spoke to them through Elsa; she had become his interpreter. He stared blankly when Tracey Harris made a reference to travelers in the snow; Elsa tried to explain and he smiled, but she could not be sure that he understood. He went off abruptly in the midst of a sentence to fling open the door of his house and beckon them inside. Elsa trooped in last, staring from the porch at the tall trees, their lower trunks hung with gray tresses of lichen. A fresh branch of pine lay on the porch and when she picked it up she experienced all over again that stirring of wonder. *When is a pine not a pine? When it grows on another planet.*

There was a corridor, narrow and dark, lit feebly by an electric bulb swinging over their heads. Kaldor had walked ahead to find more light while the others hung back. He loomed like Purkinje's specter, fitting a thick candle into a wall sconce. Elsa made up the distance and heard Dietrich speaking urgently to Harris.

"Come along — what's wrong with the place?"

So Tracey Harris was afraid of the Lodge? Elsa noted the reaction and began to look over Kaldor's living quarters more professionally. This was her last tour of duty with Welfare before she was kicked upstairs at forty-five to deal with plaintive tapes from Moon dependents.

Kaldor led the way into a cluttered, round room, solid as the tombs of Ur, lined and triple-lined with pine blocks against the stone and draped with thick hangings of kelp. There were plexiglass scraps worked into two mullioned windows; an open fireplace gave off a warm reek. A couch, covered with the familiar tan and white minto hides, swarmed into life, and two half-grown mintos the size of spaniels dove snuffling for Elsa's ankles. Kaldor gave a resounding stamp on the dirt floor and they sat back on their haunches. Elsa realized they were charming animals, like enormous chipmunks, with curious, long-lashed, yellow eyes.

The wonder was not that anyone should keep these "giant rodents" as pets but that the colonists apparently slaughtered them in droves.

"What do they eat?"

"Everything!" Kaldor gave a gusty laugh. "Lichen, kelp, meat, bones . . . my last pair of long johns."

Lieutenant Harris came in, subdued, and sat by the fire with Dietrich, stroking the little beasts.

Kaldor led Elsa to a window and she gazed with a sense of dislocation at his workbench. He had a generator, evidently, but many of his graphs were done by candlelight. He worked in longhand with pen and ink. Thick tallow candles lined the bench in hollowed cups of bone; the tallow had splashed and hardened on the stone inkwells. There were bunches of wooden pens and others whittled into stubs. The minuscule black hieroglyphics flowed over every inch of parchment. The paper and card were used up, but there was plenty of parchment in neat yellow rolls, awaiting Kaldor's industry. She reached out to feel the texture of a fresh roll but Kaldor took her hand.

"You were sent, of course," he said.

He had always been slightly paranoid; the man who assumed that all houses were bugged, when it was civilization that was bugging him. Oh, but to have to explain, to worry away at a marvelous coincidence!

"I am making a routine inspection of living conditions at the base," said Elsa firmly. "I had no idea you were on this planet."

His grin radiated pure, delighted disbelief.

"Never mind," he said. "Look at the charts."

He reached over the table and flicked down a finely drawn map of Itys, another of Earth, the North Pacific. She got his drift at once.

"Uh-huh . . ." she said. "When do you fix the date of the new Ice Age — back home?"

"Lake Agassiz will reestablish within ten years." She almost believed him; a snow goose walked over her grave. Remember the Red River Valley? An arctic landscape, where the blizzard whines and men prowl like wolves. . . . She reached out and pulled the third map down by its long hair tassel. Itys again; the northern continent marked red in a dozen places from the base to the Lodge and far north on the giant Scott glacier. Kaldor stood back with some pride.

"You must know," he said, "that I am funded by the Franklin Institute. The work includes survival techniques."

"Your rescues!" The note of enthusiasm in her voice rang false. She felt the need to please and placate Kaldor, as if he were a child.

Suddenly Dietrich cried out behind her. Tracey Harris was distressed, gasping for breath; her pretty face was stiff and drawn.

"Some kind of seizure. . . ." Dietrich had the girl by the shoulders. "Captain . . . has she done this before?" White-faced and retching, Harris staggered to her feet, her eyes fixed on Elsa.

"Alert . . . Captain!" she gasped and fell.

Dietrich and Elsa rushed to her side.

"Water!" said Elsa.

She wanted to give the M.O. something to do. She had never seen Harris so powerfully affected before but she hesitated to spring the explanation on Dietrich. There were young officers in Welfare who grated less on her nerves but no others combined high efficiency with a good psi rating. Elsa Blake knew that her own senses were common. What had spooked the girl? She looked at Kaldor, poor devil, keeping his distance with a bemused expression. Alone for months, now his place was invaded.

Tracey Harris was whispering, eyes closed; a confused jumble of names, objects.

"Bellknap, bracelet . . . folded together . . . Pruitt, appletree . . . flashes . . . Captain . . ."

Dietrich held his canteen of filtered water to the lieutenant's pale lips.

"Hey, she said Pruitt!"

"Is there someone called Pruitt?" asked Elsa.

"Sure." Dietrich looked up at Kaldor. "You remember, sir? He was with Ball in the helicopter . . . one of the guys who didn't make it."

Kaldor gave a sad grimace. "I didn't know their names. Only Ball, whom I returned."

"Franz, I'm sorry to intrude on you this way." Elsa felt the beginning of an unreasoning fear. She hoped Dietrich would shut up and play along. "I'm afraid Lieutenant Harris has some fever," she went on, covering the girl's cold forehead with her hand.

"No fever at all!" said Dietrich. "She's in some kind of receptive state, Captain. She said Pruitt, then Appleby. He was a tourist, geological surveyor from Procne, year before last. Maybe these names are marked down somewhere?

Then she said flashes; could be flashes of light. I'm keenly interested in this kind of study, Captain."

"Maybe shoulder flashes on a uniform," suggested Kaldor.

"That's it!" exclaimed Dietrich. "Her next word was 'Captain' . . . that was Appleby's rank."

"Poor child," said Kaldor; "she is a witch. What will she come out with next? My recipe for goulash . . . eh, Elsa?"

"We'll take her back to base," said Elsa.

"Please . . ." said Kaldor mildly. "I will lose my visitors too soon."

Elsa Blake stood up, dusting the knees of her trousers. Her panic had subsided.

"The lieutenant needs fresh air at any rate," she said. "Doctor, have you called the base? We're overdue."

"No sweat," said Dietrich.

He picked Tracey up in his arms, where she stirred comfortably; her cheeks were regaining their color.

"No need to call in, Captain," he said cheerfully. "We're not due back until fourteen hundred."

"Come," said Kaldor, "I'll make coffee. Bring the poor girl to the summer sleeping room. Plenty of fresh air." He gave Elsa a conspiratorial wink and guided Dietrich out of the room.

She was left alone with the lieutenant's jumble of words going through her head. Kaldor was mad, Harris was in a trance, Dietrich was stupid, she was stupid herself. She sat by the fire and stroked the young mintos; they nibbled her fingers. She got up and thumbed through Kaldor's greasy collection of cassette books. His tastes were predictable:

besides scientific texts he read anthropology and exploration. The South Seas, Antarctica, the Andes . . . an Icelandic saga, a pioneering epic poem from the twentieth century. There was a plan of the house glued to the workbench; from this original stone igloo he had built on three other beehive chambers: kitchen, workshop, summer sleeping room. There was a deep cellar with a cold store and the generator hut.

His filing system was haphazard, in a pine box. She dipped in and came up with a handful of faded Land snaps: herself and Mick; Mawson base; a tall man in an ice cave. "Bellknap Victoria Land 45." A stack of parchment folders — he used no plastic — odd separate assortments of papers, Welfare and credit disks, a missal, a long, stainless steel pin. She felt guilty and diappointed when the mintos cocked their ears: Kaldor was coming back.

Her dissatisfaction spread to the room itself; a vile place, she decided, primitive and dirty. She wanted to tear it to pieces and find whatever it was that Kaldor was hiding. She knew it was all there, all the information she needed, staring her in the face. Kaldor came in balancing two steaming mugs and a plate of lumpy, yellowish biscuits. In a checkered shirt he looked more civilized; his gaunt face was alive with excitement.

"I call these corn dodgers," he said. "Here in the cold everything keeps well."

He sat on a three-legged stool and stirred up the fire.

"Food of the pioneers," said Elsa.

He took a sip of coffee; she did the same.

"I am a pioneer," said Kaldor.

He crammed a dodger into his mouth and washed it down noisily with the coffee.

"Cornmeal, fat, salt," he said. "For a change I put in brown sugar. I have everything. They send it to me."

"Franz . . . who was Bellknap?"

"Wait, wait," he said. "Here, have one, take a bite."

The dodger tasted heavy but good.

"Bellknap has made me an exile," said Kaldor. "He is one reason. There, that wasn't so bad, my cooking? Oh Elsa, to see you, to see an old friend . . ."

"I know," she said. "But you've done so much. You've done wonders. Take a furlough."

He shook his head. "It is understood that I shall never return."

"Why not?"

"I am persona non grata. My work is acceptable, my presence is" — he sawed the air with his hand "— an embarrassment."

He turned aside a little and stared into the fire.

"Surely Mick told you about my Antarctic adventure."

"Not much." She wondered why not. "You suffered from exposure . . . had to stick it out for a while."

"Ten weeks," said Kaldor. "Dave Bellknap, myself. He died at once. I survived . . . by means of him. Do you understand? I put myself forever apart from the race."

Elsa felt an immense compassion and relief. It was enough. A bad experience that he had turned into a rationale for his exile. Even the rescues were an expiation of guilt.

"Franz. . . ." She laid a hand on his shoulder. "You're the

same man . . . this is in the past. The Franklin people can't expect you to remain here indefinitely."

"Oh, I understood them," said Kaldor. "They pay me to stay away. I am a remittance man."

"What do they pay you?"

"Supplies," he said. "Chance rescues. Visitors."

He poured more coffee but Elsa took a tour of the room. She had an image of a pebble rolling down a snowy slope, becoming larger and larger as more snow packed around it.

"Elsa. . . ." Kaldor was watching her very closely. "I have learned total survival. Nothing to be wasted."

"You get a lot of native products," she said. "Kelp . . . and the mintos. . . ."

Hides and tallow, she had been going to say. A snowball . . . a ball of wax. She reached out for a roll of parchment; her gorge still did not rise. She strolled back to the fireplace and deliberately ate the last corn dodger. Cornmeal, salt, fat.

"How are the others?" she asked.

"I put them to sleep . . ." he whispered. "The girl sees too much."

Their faces were close together; she could see the broken veins on his cheeks, the pores of his skin. She was possessed not by revulsion but by a murderous fury. Kaldor locked his hands gently around her wrists.

"You must stay," he went on. "Share my discoveries." Elsa bent her head and let her arms slacken in his grasp.

"Think only that they flew away," he murmured. "An accident in the helicopter. Presently I will give them more drugs from the young man's bag."

"They're alive?"

"Of course. Alive. Fresh."

She brought her knee up savagely into his face, broke her wrists free, and shoved him clumsily into the fireplace. He came after her very fast, bleeding and singed. She was a head taller, but hand to hand her techniques were rusty; she knew she was no match for him. Her only advantage was ferocity. She flung the heavy pine box at him, waist high. As Kaldor staggered she plucked a squealing minto into the air by the scruff of its neck and heaved it, clawing wildly, into his face. She dived into the corridor, completely dark now, and ran, in nightmare, remembering the plan. She heard Kaldor blunder out of the round room, calling her name.

Elsa felt along the walls until she came to the opening—no door, only a double curtain of minto hide. The summer sleeping room was bare and bright; it would remain this way for two months with only a few hours shadow when Procne eclipsed the Star. Tracey Harris lay on an old sleeping bag stuffed with pine needles; Dietrich, bound securely at wrists and ankles, was curled on the floor. They were sleeping heavily.

Elsa realized that she had made an error of judgment. Neither of her companions had any hidden weapons. Kaldor could trap her here like a mother with her children; a knife at their throats and she was powerless. The object of the exercise was to draw him off. Dietrich groaned at her feet; she knelt down and shook him.

"Doctor . . . alert!"

He groaned so loudly that she put her hand over his mouth. His eyes focused.

"Captain . . ." he murmured.

She pleaded with him urgently: ". . . blaster, laser . . . any sidearms at all?"

His eyes were glazing over. "Pentam caps . . ." he slurred. "In . . . coffee. . . ."

Kaldor called out, very close. "*Elsa*!"

"Lie still," she whispered to Dietrich.

He raised his head an inch from the floor.

"Gun . . ." he said. "Inna chopper. . . ."

He faded again. She went out over the wide stone windowsill and edged past the wooden shutters on the warm outer wall. She heard Kaldor enter the sleeping room, call her name, and pass on. Then she was among the pines, sprinting from tree to tree. Her head suddenly became clear. She stood still among the tall trees under the pale sky of Itys. She was released from the dark tumulus of Kaldor's house; she was refreshed, single-minded.

She plunged for the helicopter and clambered into the cabin. When she had the rotors spinning she realized that the order was wrong; she should have looked for the gun first. Keeping a close watch on the Lodge she found the gun in a rack behind the back seat. It was a small-caliber repeating rifle; a sporting gun for shooting mintos. She took two clips and loaded confidently. Still Kaldor did not come out of his house. She realized nothing but the matter at hand and the resinous tang of the pine trees. She climbed down again and ran back to the encircling pines on the other side of the clearing.

Kaldor ran out of the house waving his arms and shouting.

He carried a stun-gun; she knew he would be reluctant to hurt her. She was closer now, behind a stout, bearded tree; the lichen was fine as human hair. She shouted and waved, her voice lost in the sound of the rotors.

"Franz . . . over here. . . ."

He caught sight of her and gestured clumsily with the stun-gun. He was shouting, pleading as he came toward her tree. Her concentration was excellent. He fell down on the fourth shot; she shot him twice more as he lay on the ground. Then she raced back to the chopper and killed the switches.

She sat in the pilot's seat, attempting to process all the data. She was in limbo: she had been absolutely convinced of the necessity to shoot that man but the theory of what he had done or threatened to do remained unproved and vague. Tears began to run down her cheeks; she was at a loss to explain them. Presently she climbed down again and went to look at his body. Yes, it was Franz Kaldor; a stirring of the old compulsion told her that she had done very well . . . one shot had penetrated his right eye, from how far? Fifteen meters. She had never been much of a marksman. She covered his head with her own parka and remained kneeling in shadow, breathing in the fragrance of the pines.

She had the theory but no proof. Yes, she was alone, but Itys seemed such a good place in summer; she could wander off into the pine woods, lose herself, become a recluse. Was this how every murderer felt? The pines must be taken into account . . . aided concentration, reinforced neurosis . . . a drug that encouraged fanaticism. . . . She remembered the others in their drugged sleep. She was concerned for them and struggled wearily to her feet.

She went back into the Lodge, carrying the gun although she knew there were no enemies in the house. She looked into the round room; the mintos were asleep by the dying fire. She felt numb and queasy at the sight of the tallow candles. She fumbled for her own small flashlight in the pocket of her tunic and lit her way to the summer sleeping room. Tracey Harris was still asleep but Dietrich was stirring again. Elsa took out her clasp knife and cut the thongs around his wrists and ankles. He forced himself awake.

"That guy . . ." he said. "Captain?"

"He won't bother you," she said.

". . . Killed those tourists . . . in the snow . . ." he murmured. "Tracey said so."

"That's what he did all right."

Elsa Blake was aching and sick. She was tempted to wait until Dietrich could come along. He crawled over beside Harris and checked the girl's pulse. Elsa took a deep breath, picked up a twig of green pine from the mattress, and went out again. She went down toward the hum of the generator. She found a bank of lights at the first landing on the stairs; the storerooms were well lit. There was a distinctive odor but no smell of carrion or decay; the rooms were very cold. She walked down stiffly into the cold, feeling the muscles pull behind her knees.

She did not examine the barrels and boxes, the tubs of lard and cooking fat. She glanced at the scrubbed butcher's block and the surgical array of steel knives. Then, with clenched teeth, she dragged open the door of Kaldor's freezing chamber. She saw the neat hanging rows of flayed haunches, trunks, and limbs, swathed in gauze or yellow skin-parchment. She looked long enough to make sure . . . eight or ten . . . men and women. . . . A smaller package made Elsa Blake draw in her breath sharply but it contained only the carcass of a young minto.

Science fiction has always demonstrated a dark awareness of the catastrophes that could destroy civilization: nuclear holocausts, worldwide plagues, insect mutations, and even the sun's going nova have decimated our cities and technology in many a story. But short of every human on Earth being suddenly killed, there's only one thing that can truly destroy us . . . as Robert Bloch shows in this pungent short-short.

Robert Bloch has been a major name in the fields of science fiction and horror writing for forty years. He won a Hugo Award for his short story *That Hell-Bound Train,* and his novel *Psycho* is recognized as a classic of modern horror.

The Head

Robert Bloch

ONE MORNING, when Jon was ten years old, it was raining too hard for him to go out and kill anybody.

He stood at the top of the cave looking out at the storm, telling himself rain was a goodie, man. But he felt kind of, you know, down.

So Jon stash the knife away under the belt of his jock and went back into the tunnels to find somebody he could do it to. Only he coulden catch any of the little kids because they run when they see him coming. And he know if he wassen careful some of the biggies would do it to him.

He diden turn on for that, not even when Grope did it, but at lease Grope kepp the others offen him. Grope was the biggest stud in the whole cave, and he never let anyone do it to his old ladies or his kids excep himself.

The hangup was, Grope had went away on a skull-hunt with the gang and Jon didden trust the others. Even though it was raining the women was out in the fields and the kids was running loose all through the cave with their knives and clubs, hassling. Moving along, Jon could hear the noises from out of the side tunnels — laughs and screams and moans.

So Jon kepp to the middle of the big cave where the cooking fires light up the way. Each gang had their own, with a creep watching to see it never went out. Creeps were like too old to hunt or work in the fields and they coulden do it anymore, so most of them just got killed, but they was always a few leff to keep the fires.

The kids never went to the cooking fires alone. Jon remember one time he was little, Grope find a kid try to rip off food from a pot. Grope juss pick the kid up and smash her brains out on the side of a rock. So she end up in the cookpot herself. All the other kids laugh, ha ha, but they diden forget. And after that they kepp away from the fires excepp at feeding times.

Thass why it was safe to stay in the big cave now, but Jon was itchy, he wannet to do something. So he grab a torch and went down into Grope's side tunnel very slow and careful in case someone hide there. But the tunnel was empty and he crepp down in the dark until he pass the sleeping-place and find the entrance hole to the burrows way farther on. There was lotsa burrows twisty all through the rock and Jon know his way good. Nobody else ever come this far.

They was rocks falled into the tunnels, too many for the biggies to climb over, but Jon start to crawl through when he was a little kid and he was the only one ever. Thass how come he find the secret place.

The secret place was far under. Jon went through falled rocks to where the walls was, you know, all smooth. Not rocks, the walls, but something else. Like his knife—hard and shiny. And then he went to where they was the buzz noise.

When he first went there the buzz noise scare him, but he got use to it after while. It never hurt him, only noise from somewhere behind the smooth walls. So now he kepp on to where he diden need a torch because they was light. The light come from somewhere behind like the buzz.

Nobody know about the buzz or the light and Jon never tole because that was part of the secret.

The secret was in a little smooth-wall cave with more buzz noise and light blinks from under a shelf with knobs in it. Jon remember how it scare him long time ago to see the big shiny bubble on the shelf, like he tried to smash it with a rock but the rock just bounce off. Then he twist knobs and they diden come loose, but more light come from the shiny bubble so he could see what was inside.

That was the real secret, like floating inside the bubble with the long thin things sticking down out of the ears and neck.

A big head, all wrinkle and hairy. Eyes shut tight, mouth shut too. Dead.

Until Jon twist knobs like he done the first time. Now the sparks jump from long thin things.

The eyes open, look at him. The mouth open too.

And the head say, "Good morning, Jon."

Good morning, Jon.

He could hear his voice say it, but maybe it wasn't really morning: time had no meaning here. And it wasn't really his voice — just the level, artificial output of the mechanism powered by the feeble electrical impulse of his tongue and laryngeal nerve; electronically amplified, as was his hearing.

What was the old phrase? *Damned clever, these Chinese.* Inappropriate, of course. The Chinese hadn't perfected this variation of the crionics technique; in fact it had been arrived at just prior to the threatened thermonuclear holocaust. They'd anticipated the results, and this was the solution. A chemical solution, in which the brain was preserved and electrically reactivated.

It was the only way they'd come up with. They couldn't save the atmosphere, they couldn't save the artifacts, they couldn't save human life. But perhaps, under these conditions, they could save knowledge.

They reasoned that recorded knowledge is perishable — books and tapes and microfilms are subject to disintegration.

Or, even if preserved, to misinterpretation. And computers weren't the answer; perpetual power couldn't be generated or maintained on a sufficient scale for maintainence of large units, and they'd be useless to anyone without sophisticated training.

The one sure source of wisdom was still the mind. So select the minds, select the precious few who were psychologically suitable to withstand such stress and preserve them. Place them in the strategically situated security bunkers far below the surface, and hook them up to the self-maintained mechanisms of input and output. Sooner or later someone would find them. There would be survivors; eventually the atmosphere would shed itself of pollution. Then the remnants of the human race, ready for regeneration, would stumble across the secret storage-spots, the secret sources of science and skill and scholarship that were waiting to rebuild a new world from the ruins.

That had been the plan. There were other minds buried away in various top-security subterranea; maybe they hadn't been discovered yet, maybe they never would be discovered. But the law of averages, the law of accident, had led to this resurrection.

I am the resurrection and the life, saith the Lord. And a little child shall lead them. A child, prowling the caves and chancing upon this unit, fumbling with the unfamiliar gadgetry, reactivating his awareness.

He stared at the creature crouching before him. Blurry, indistinct, out of focus. *Better correct that.*

"Jon — can you hear me?"

The crouching figure nodded.

"Good. Now listen carefully. Remember what I told you the other times you came here — about the switches?"

The creature blinked. Something was puzzling him. *Switch.* He didn't understand the word. What term would he know?

"The *knob*, Jon. The knob on the left."

The creature nodded again, and reached forward.

"There. Push it up. Slow — not too far — just a little way. That's better."

Yes, he could see clearly now. But *was* it better? Was it really better to get a clear glimpse of this near-naked figure — this white ape? Not even white, actually, but a new ethnic admixture of Caucasian and Negroid, a product of generations of inbreeding here in the doomed darkness.

Their previous confrontations had produced little more than knowledge of Jon's name; his people had no history, no consciousness of continuity. As far as Jon was aware, they had always lived in the caves, always scratched and scrabbled on the scarred surface just outside and above to find weeds for the cook-pots, always hunted other groups from other caves to supplement their daily diet with occasional meat. They had fire, shelter, crude weapons, a surviving semblance of an urban subculture based upon the concept of gangs and territories. This much he had learned through patient questioning, and perhaps there was no more. *Savages.*

He dismissed the thought; it wasn't important. What mattered now was that this creature was all that remained of humanity. The hope of the future, the sole surviving hope.

It could speak. "Tell me something, man."

Man. This creature was mankind, what was left of it. Shorn of heritage, stripped of civilization, its language reduced to crude slang.

God, how could he educate *this*? How could he even communicate clearly? But he had to, he must, it was the only way.

"Like talk, man."

So he talked.

Once again, just as he had so many times before, he told Jon the story. Told him of the old days, the days of innocence before the wars, when people walked proud and free over the face of the earth and built their shining cities with spires thrusting high into the heavens; built their shining hopes still higher, soaring to the stars.

That's what it was to Jon — a story. He was listening, he always listened, but obviously he didn't believe. Any more than humanity had believed in the Garden of Eden.

In a way, of course, this new world *was* the Garden of Eden he talked about — Earth in the day before the Fall. And the growing dissent that had led to the war — the racial, political, religious, ideological, sexist strife with its breakdown of communications on every level — had been like the Tower of Babel. Just as the final war itself was like the Flood, wiping out the world. Its survivors didn't land on a mountaintop; instead they were inside the mountain. The children of Noah, crouching in this cave.

He listened to himself — to the mechanical output of his thought — and recognized how much it all sounded like a fairy tale. That's the way the biblical accounts had sounded to him in the old days. Fables, fantasies, folklore. If it had been difficult for him to conceive of the simplicity of the Garden of Eden, how much harder must it be for Jon to realize the reality of a complicated civilization.

And yet it was true. There *had* been hope for a heaven on earth, until humanity turned it into hell. For most, hell had been a shockingly swift and short nightmare of fear and pain, followed by merciful oblivion. But the true meaning of hell had been revealed to only a few, like himself. He knew what hell really was.

Hell was forever.

Hell was a darkness that never died, a nightmare that never ended. Hell was the fear and pain of being alive and aware in that darkness, utterly isolated, unable to see or hear or speak or even move. Hell was being alone with his thoughts forever; thoughts that never slept, thoughts that echoed eternally with a soundless shrieking that shattered the skull.

That was *his* hell, before Jon turned him on. And that was his hell when Jon turned him off and left him alone in the dark.

So now it didn't really matter if Jon believed him or not, just as long as he was willing to listen. Because if Jon was listening he wouldn't turn him off.

Keep talking, keep him interested. Tell him about anything, everything. About radar, lasers, fission, fusion, super- and subsonics, microcosm, macrocosm, dactyls and pterodactyls, all the wonders and blunders of the world. "And then, Jon, we started to conquer space. We landed on the moon —"

"You tole that." Jon scowled; he was bored. "Tell about big kills."

Big kills. The war. He didn't want to talk about the war; that was Privileged Information, Top Security, the sealed orders and the directive that had sent him here to the Classified Area. Operation Survival—that's what they'd labeled it, the procedure that placed him under the knife at the very last moment when the earth shuddered and the mountaintop melted over his head. But he'd obeyed, they'd all obeyed; scientists and surgeons sweating as they wielded their scalpels under the sizzling, sputtering lights before the final darkness. Their words came back to him. "*But damn it, don't you understand? It isn't death — you'll be alive! There's bound to be someone who finds you sooner or later and when they do, when they turn on the power, you'll be reborn. And so will the human race — reborn with the knowledge you retain.*"

That was the hope he had taken down with him into the darkness, the purpose that had sustained him in the hideous, endless emptiness.

But that's not what Jon wanted to hear about. He was scowling again, scratching his armpit.

"More kill," Jon said. "Boms. You know, man."

"I *don't* know," he said. "And you don't know, either. You're not a man — you're a child. That's why you must listen to me, listen and learn. There's more to life than killing and feeding and copulation. If you listen I can teach you."

"Tell how you make bom." Jon grinned. "Someday I kill Grope."

"No, that's not the way."

Jon shook his head stubbornly. "Tell me!"

Tell him what? Where were the words, how could he reach him, teach him, save him from savagery, lead his people out of the wilderness?

And whose words would serve — those of Jesus, Buddha, Muhammad, Lao-tse, Plato, Spinoza, Confucius, Shakespeare? What prophets, priests, philosophers, savants, or sages in the history of mankind could show him the solution?

He had to find those words now, for Jon's sake, for his own sake, if only to keep from being turned off again, from being turned back into that ceaseless silence, that blind blackness. A brain, buried alive beneath a mountain.

Mountain. Wilderness. Hadn't Moses led a nomad rabble into a wilderness, climbed a mountain? Suppose the biblical Babel and Flood were allegories. Suppose there had been thermonuclear destruction then — and the same solution? Scientists of a forgotten civilization had hit upon the secret of salvation, preserved a living intelligence against the day when some primitive survivor would encounter it, hidden away and waiting to bring the light of truth back into the world. Suppose Moses had gone into the mountain, found just such a cave, stumbled across just such a mechanism, turned it on, and heard the voice of God?

Steady, now. God wouldn't dread the darkness the way he dreaded it, God wouldn't feel the fear of being turned off. *You're not God, remember that.*

But you can be God's voice.

You can be God's voice and Jon can be Moses. Speak to

him in God's words, so that he can lead his people to the Promised Land.

"Thou shalt not kill," he said.

Jon frowned at him, shaking his head. "I kill Grope. You see."

"No. Grope is your father. Honor thy father and thy mother — don't you understand?"

Jon grimaced, his eyes restless, resentful. He wasn't interested.

But there had to be a way! A way to save Jon and the others, a way to save himself. Because if he was turned off once again he knew he would truly go mad, finally and irrevocably mad, and there would be no voice of God, only the writhing and wriggling and crazed clawing within his bursting brain alone in the darkness and foreverness. There would be darkness over the heavens and the earth, and without his voice, God would be dead.

Jon was reaching for the knob now. Reaching, bored and impatient.

He was powerless to prevent it. Only God had that power. Salvation. Salvation through prayer. *Yes, that was the way.*

He spoke then. Spoke the only words that would save the world, the words that never failed, the words of wisdom, the words of the ages, the words of God.

"The Lord is my shepherd: I shall not want. He maketh me to lie down in green pastures; he leadeth me beside the still waters. He restoreth my soul —"

Jon was listening now. Did he understand? Was there

enough humanity left in this creature to comprehend the truth? The answer would decide his fate forever, Jon's fate, the fate of the world, the fate of God.

Then Jon smiled and the answer came.

"That's shit, man," Jon said.

And turned him off.

The dangers of experimentation with nuclear power have become a subject of major controversy lately, and for good reason: we're dealing with awesome forces when we try to harness the power of the atom. Science fiction has produced innumerable cautionary stories on this subject — a classic early example was Lester del Rey's *Nerves* (1942) — and now Alan Brennert brings the problem into tight personal focus in a deceptively understated tale of a family living in the dark shadow of nuclear horror.

Alan Brennert is a graduate of the Clarion Science Fiction Writers' Workshop; his stories have appeared in many sf magazines and anthologies, and he was nominated in 1975 for the John W. Campbell Award as the best new sf writer of the year.

Jamie's Smile

Alan Brennert

Birthdays are for dying once a year; more often and it's no longer a merry thing. So while my own would pass in a flurry of half-glimpsed Hallmarks, my nephew Jamie's became the focus of my family's masochistic attentions. Some innate sense of proportion allowed them but one sacrificial lamb, and Jamie, God help him, was it.

Once a year, then, I would bundle myself up, hop a bus or

hitch a ride, and make my birthday pilgrimage to L.A. And once a year I would find myself at my brother Walter's apartment, shrugging off my coat in a dim foyer, and with it any pretense of being a stranger here.

On the eleventh pilgrimage my mother looked much as she had on the previous ten: thin, bony, very probably more active at sixty-eight than I at thirty-two, her pinched features dry as old parchment. I pecked her on the cheek and hung my jacket on a rather ugly coatrack. "Who died and left you this?" I said.

"That? It was in the old house. Walter went over a few months ago for a last look, to see if there was anything in the attic rooms that might be salvageable."

"If that's what he salvaged I'd hate to see what he deep-sixed." Our family has an unnatural love for the art of reclamation.

"How are you, Judson?"

"Emphysemic," I said. "Between the buses and the smog I'll probably never breathe again."

"You'll find it a hard habit to break. Walter," she called into the living room, "Walter, Judson is here."

We walked into the living room and I noted with a silent resignation that it had not changed much since last year: the overstuffed furniture, the piss-yellow wallpaper, and of course my brother Walt, the oldest and grayest of its features, today looking more uncomfortable than usual in a vest two sizes too small.

"Jud!" We shook hands; his palm was cold and damp, like dead flesh. "How the hell are you. Drink?"

"No, no thanks, Walt."

"Oh hell, that's right," he said, going to the bar. They don't touch it in Laguna, do they? Sorry," he added with a small laugh, "can't offer you pot or anything. . . ."

"Don't be silly, Walter," my mother said. "You know Judson doesn't go in for that sort of thing."

Walt shrugged. "Well, it's been a year and all. *I* don't know."

I felt the old knee-jerk urge come back to me, the urge to snap at my mother for tying me down to a preset mode of behavior. Walt was right, I wanted to say, a year can bring a lot of changes; but this year hadn't, damn it; Mother was right and any argument would have been absurd. I felt confined again, boxed into another's idea of what I was. My own birthday suit, as it were.

"How *are* you doing up there, anyway?" Walt asked, drinking his gin, one thumb hooked into his frayed belt. God, how he'd gained weight.

"Starving, generally."

"You don't look it," Mother said. "Or did you mean that symbolically?"

Walt laughed. "Artists have to starve, it's in their blood."

"So are low sugar levels," I said. "When do we eat, by the way?"

"After the interrogation," Becky said from behind me. "I should think you'd have learned the procedure by now." She entered the room smiling warmly, her thin sandy hair now shoulder length, longer than it had been when I last saw her. I liked it this way better.

She came and took my hands in hers, examining me with her glinting brown eyes. "Toulouse, you've grown."

"Platform knees, mademoiselle. One finds it difficult to kneel in prayer, but we must all sacrifice."

"Don't we, though?" She kissed me coolly on the cheek, then drew away. "Jamie is in the bathroom, washing his hands. He insisted on not using the i-v today."

"Insisted?" I said.

Mother said, "He's eating with us?"

Becky nodded. "Yes, he thinks he can."

"Insisted?" I repeated.

Beck shrugged lightly. "The hand-signals were rather — fierce. He stood firm." An embarrassed silence. "I mean he was adamant. Oh hell, you know what I mean."

"Of course," I said superfluously.

Walt wedged himself into the conversation: "Darling," he said to Becky, "why don't you show Jud what we got Jamie for his birthday?"

"Before he opens it?" I said.

"Oh, I think he knows what it is already," Walt said. "He's very —"

"Perceptive," Mother prompted.

"Something like that, yes."

"I'd rather wait," I said. "I got him some new books. They're in my jacket. We can give them all at once."

I can't say I usually cared very much what they had bought for Jamie. I supposed it was some art supplies, in which case it would be incumbent upon me to tutor Jamie in their use, as I had tutored him in charcoals and inks. If so, I wanted to do it, but for Jamie and not because it was expected of me.

"Then I guess we'll open them after dinner," Walt said, "if that's okay with —"

I stopped listening to Walt. The grinding whir of Jamie's wheelchair began quite suddenly, souring my stomach all at once; it continued in short staccato bursts as Jamie entered the room, the chair grinding its way across the faded tan carpet.

Jamie reminded me of half-finished sculpture, the smooth plaster mold rather than the solid bronze statue. The hand of his creator, whoever or whatever it was, had been snatched away the moment Jamie had been squeezed from between Becky's thighs. His hands were thin, delicate in a way that suggested weakness rather than artistry; there was webbing between the third and fourth fingers, and no little fingers at all, merely stumps. His feet were always covered by socks or slippers, concealing ankles of thin bone, too weak to support his weight. The flesh that covered hands and feet was stretched taut, almost translucent: beneath it could be seen the pulse and flow of capillaries, veins.

His face was much the same, but the skin was paler still, and even his lips lacked color as they lacked form. Those lips — two lines carelessly sketched on the plaster, waiting for further delineation — never parted more than half a centimeter. At least not since the moment the doctor had pulled him from Becky, slapped him on the ass, and listened as the baby tried to scream — but couldn't. His vocal cords had never developed and, in time, his facial muscles atrophied.

"Well, Jamie," Mother said, "Uncle Jud finally made it."

Uncle Jud *always* made it. Uncle Jud was feeling the same way he felt every year at this time: sick with memory and guilty for that sickness. I smiled and approached Jamie, trying to ignore the patch of sterile cloth on his neck that covered the results of a long-ago tracheotomy.

I took his hand in mine and shook it. I could feel his fingers grasping mine in what had to be an effort for him, and all at once the sickness vanished and I was with my nephew.

"Hello, Jamie," I said, releasing his hand. He nodded a greeting and a silent communion passed between us. The ritual of strangeness was over. No emotion showed on his face, but I sensed in him an almost desperate gladness to see me. To see anyone beyond the immediate family, I supposed.

"I'll get dinner ready," Mother said. "You've done enough, Becky."

"I'll go in and change, then," Becky said. "Jud, why don't you talk to Jamie awhile? Walt, clear away the junk on the dining room table."

"Anything you say, love." Walt had a habit of adding a term of endearment whenever he was being subservient. It was one of the things that grated on my nerves — that, and the way he had seemed to die in the mind years ago, the slow dissolve of morale that had let his body go to fat while his ambition went to hell.

I watched him slosh over to the dining room table and pull off the newspaper and other crap strewn over the scratched Formica top. How could a man that large look like a burst balloon? I didn't know. I think I hated him. He was everything I was trying desperately not to be, but I didn't know whether or not I was succeeding and so I hated him all the more.

And he was only four years older than I was.

I turned and looked down at Jamie, and found a knowing and an agreement in his half-shut, watery eyes.

I kneeled by his side and put my hand over one of his. "How are you, Jamie?"

Walt had been doing some minor engineering work at Edison's nuclear power plant at San Onofre. Landing a job on the initial staff was one of the few good moves he made in his life — that, and marrying Becky — and for half a year he was as happy as I'd ever seen him. For half a year he was also soaking up trace amounts of spillage, radiation falling unnoticed on flesh and seed. Edison discovered the leak before the exposure became lethal, but not before Jamie had been conceived.

Walt lost his hair, grew it back, developed cataracts and had them removed at the company's expense. Edison agreed to pay some piddling compensation and Walter, being Walter, accepted the offer. They didn't suggest aborting the child until it became apparent that it might actually live. But Walt was quite effectively sterile from that time on, and the doctors were saying that Becky should not attempt to have any more children after what was sure to be a difficult birth — or a difficult abortion. And they both *wanted* children. Confused, shaken, they decided to chance it.

Horror stories circulated in the family that fall, forgotten deformities from all branches of the family tree brought to new light in the atomic glare. For my part I had stray visions of fetus and embryo, saw Walt in a plane flying silent above Nagasaki, kneeling beside a bomb dropping through irising bay doors. And then the bombs would fall, becoming small and blurred and soft, and Walt would continue to kneel there, slamming them home to target, driving, driving. . . .

If it had been Jamie and Jamie alone, an afternoon or a weekend of teaching him how to use those pale hands for something besides writing brief, functional notes in lieu of speech — if it had been that, I would not have minded. Instead, it was Walt and Becky and my mother, celebrating a birth they would rather damn — that was what I hated. That was what I feared, in my selfish way, all year.

I escaped into the bathroom a minute, and as I came out I passed Jamie's bedroom. I noticed that his bed was closer to the window now, almost flush with the wall. The room was still painted a sickly green with cream trim: my mother's doing, I recalled. My mother, once a registered nurse, now Jamie's nurse, couldn't help turning this room into a hospital ward. My gaze fell on the i-v stand tucked away in a corner, its long tube falling in a languid loop to the floor.

There were quite a few new books; one entire wall was obscured by shelves of glossy paperbacks and worn hardcovers, frayed-edged magazines and torn, yellowed newspaper clippings. Jamie loved to read: novels, news stories, philosophy, pornography . . . anything that spoke of a world beyond his narrow universe. I knew the feeling.

I went into the kitchen where Mother was juggling dishes and pans. The odor of steamed fish permeated the room; on one burner a soft, whitish concoction that looked like baby food bubbled obscenely.

I nodded toward it. "That for Jamie?"

Mother grabbed a saucepan with a pot holder. "Yes, it's a vegetable concentrate. He eats it sometimes, for the sake of eating something. Through a straw; he can manage that. My God, it must be awful to have to take all your food through that damned tube."

"It must be difficult for him to do otherwise. You're sure he really wants to make the effort and join us?"

"Don't be silly, dear, of course he does. These parties are as special to him as they are to us. Did you see the way he smiled when he saw you?"

I suppressed a weary sigh. "Mother, Jamie can't smile."

"Well of course he can. He can smile with his eyes. You can see it in the way he looks at you . . . the way he watches what's happening."

"Have you seen that — smile — very often?"

She poured some steaming water into the sink, her back to me. "Every . . . once in a while, yes," she said. Her voice was odd and I felt she was deliberately keeping her face from me.

"Well, I'm glad to hear that," I said. Not believing her for a minute. Perhaps Jamie *had* smiled on seeing me — but why would he ever have occasion to smile at any other time, here, with them, caged?

Mother turned abruptly and faced me, her eyes hard, almost fanatical. "Things have worked out very well for Jamie. You were wrong when you thought they wouldn't. He may be a cripple, but he can do things and be happy. The art, he loves the art. And his books." She turned back to the sink and dropped the pan into the basin with a sharp clang. "And to think that bitch wanted him dead. Thank God Walter didn't listen."

She went over to the stove to turn off the oven, the fierceness gone from her eyes. "Better go inside, Judson, dinner will be ready in a few minutes."

I hesitated a moment, then backed out of the kitchen. I had never become used to my mother's flares of cold temper, those icy novas that burned briefly in her eyes, then faded. They always took me by surprise.

In the dining room Becky was setting the table. Off somewhere I heard the grind and hum of Jamie's wheelchair, and the rattle of ice cubes in Walt's glass.

Becky smiled at my entrance but did not look up. "Well, Toulouse, have you finished inspecting the Bastille?"

"Oh God damn it, Becky, knock it off. If it's that much of a prison, get out. Stop banging your wine glass against the bars." I was surprised by my own vehemence. So was Becky; she looked up and stared at me.

She smiled grimly. "Sorry. But who else is going to listen, Jud?"

I sighed and wrapped my arms loosely about her waist in what I hoped was friendly in-law fashion. "Beck, Beck . . . damn it, I'm always listening. You're the one who turns a deaf ear." Her arms encircled my own waist, her fingers gently finding the small of my back; despite myself I began to run my hands along her thighs, along the tight seam of her skirt, the touch and rhythm of it all-too-suddenly familiar. I fought to keep myself from getting hard, I fought to remind myself why this could never work. "Becky, I —"

I didn't notice Walt's approach until he had entered the room. He paused in the doorway, blinked once, and for a moment I thought I saw a pale fire in his eyes.

Becky and I disengaged ourselves, but Walt was already leaving. "Sorry," he said tonelessly. "I'm sure you two have things to talk about." He disappeared into the foyer leading to the bathroom.

I watched him go, suddenly angry. "Jesus!" I said to Becky. "That's what you don't want to leave? That *shadow*? My God, he's just like Mother. For a moment they allow themselves anger or rage, then they damp the fires and turn to ash."

"I can't leave Jamie, can I?" Her face was impassive — a trick she'd learned from them, no doubt. "And I can't support him by myself. He needs someone to look after him constantly; Mother does that here, but she'd hardly come with me, would she? A nurse costs money, Jud, and I'm not trained for anything more than steno."

"Then just get the hell out. Leave them, the three of them. Edison still pays you some compensation benefits, don't they? Walt could make up the difference for medical costs, and Mother could go on tending to Jamie. And you'd be free."

She stared at me a second. "Walt hasn't worked in nine months," she said quietly. "Even before that I had to bring in something to add to those glorious benefits. That something grew larger and larger every month. Now it's everything. I'm the support around here, I'm the foundation, not Walt, not anybody else."

I didn't know what to say. "I — my God, Beck, I didn't know —"

She laughed shortly, not a nice laugh. "No, of course you didn't. How much of a damn do you give for us? Once a year is all you have to suffer. You tell me to get the hell out; all right, if I do, will you give up your days and watch Jamie? Or go to work to support his i-v, his chair, the whole thing? Can you divorce yourself from your damned artists' colony as easily as you have from your fami —"

She stopped suddenly, as if hearing herself for the first time. She sank into one of the dining room chairs and lowered her eyes.

"Oh God," she said. "I'm sorry, Jud. You're free and I'm trying to make you feel guilty about it." She looked up, tried to smile. "Forget I said anything, will you?"

I nodded. "It's forgotten." But she was right, damn it. I'd tried to divorce them from my life, all of them, but could anyone ever annul his own past?

"But do you see —" She watched me, seeking absolution. "You do see how it is? I can't give up on Jamie. We brought him into this world, God help us, and we owe him for that. Responsibility, damn it; it wasn't his fault, it was mine, mine for not being strong enough to refuse the tracheotomy. Does that sound awful? Maybe it is. But it would've been better for all of us if Jamie had never found a way to breathe. For once in my life I was weak, and for once in his life Walt was strong, and we were both so damned wrong."

She stood up, trying to regain that lost impassivity that

Walt and Mother so loved. She took my hands again. "Weird relatives you have, eh, Toulouse?"

"No," I said. "Weird family I have."

She smiled at the word. I smiled at having said it.

And from the kitchen Mother called out that dinner was ready. "Give me hand, Becky. Walt? Jamie? Jud?"

Jamie sat between Walt (at the head of the table) and Becky (to Jamie's left), holding between his middle fingers a spindly straw. I sat opposite him, Mother opposite Becky. No one said grace; as I've said, my family has an innate sense of proportion, and the saying of grace would have tipped the delicate balance of irony.

Jamie nursed that straw of his like a child at the breast, sucking that dreadful cream-of-crapola slowly but forcefully from the shallow dish. I kept my gaze down, making a careful study of the bone china plates I ate from. Eating became something of a ritual as I tried to avoid watching Jamie, and I was almost grateful for the tepid questioning that went on throughout the meal.

Mother: "What have you been working on recently, Judson?"

Me: "Nothing, I'm afraid. Haven't felt right about anything. For a while there I thought I might do some sculpture, but —"

Walt: "How do you survive if you don't produce regularly? Not that I'm criticizing; hell —"

Me: "I manage. I still have some of the cash I got from that portrait commission a while back."

Mother: "A while back! Seven months. And how much, only two, three hundred dollars?"

I was about to say that I didn't need much, about to become argumentative, when I became aware of Jamie's hand; he had moved it toward a pitcher of milk and it was abruptly in my field of vision. I felt a momentary shock and a subsequent guilt over it; the hand — I almost thought of it as separate from Jamie — the hand was vainly trying to reach the distant pitcher.

Walt reached for it. "Here, Jamie, I'm closer." Jamie withdrew his hand, knocking over the sugar bowl and spilling its contents over the tablecloth. Becky sighed heavily.

"Don't sweat it," Walt said, and clumsily extended his reach to try to right the bowl; but his slow, uncoordinated arms succeeded only in knocking over Jamie's dinner dish, spilling the vegetable concentrate into Becky's lap.

I stared. Jamie blinked. "Oh shit, Beck, I'm sorrry," Walt stammered. "Here, let me —"

Becky stood up, allowing the creamed vegetable crap to drip onto the carpet. Walt grabbed a napkin and went to her side, tried to wipe the stuff from her skirt, but Becky recoiled at his touch. Her eyes burned with brief resentment.

"Keep your fucking hands to yourself, will you," she snapped, wiping the cream from her leg herself. "You've done enough as it is." She turned and headed toward the bathroom, leaving Walt standing there, uncertain, embarrassed. I felt a horrible pity for him at that moment, the pity one feels for a lost animal and not at all the pity one should feel for a human being. I didn't like the feeling.

Walt put the napkin down on the table, looked at Jamie as

if remembering something, and then moved the pitcher of milk nearer to his son's arm.

"Here you are, Jamie," he said absently. "Excuse me, Jud? Mother?"

He too left the room, heading in the general direction of the bar. Mother was already up and brushing the sugar off the table and into her cupped hand. Jamie started his wheelchair and went into his bedroom; I got up and followed Walt into the living room, something familiar tugging at my mind.

He was making a drink, of course, the hands preparing it trembling like fallen branches. I felt uncomfortable; I felt the gap between us, wide and deep; and for the first time in how long, I wasn't sure if I wanted that gap there.

I joined him at the bar. "I, uh — I'll have that drink now, if you would," I said, the words taking me by surprise as much as they did Walt. I saw something stir in his eyes, a kind of foggy pleasure — that someone would share something with him? I don't know.

"Sure," he said, managing a crippled smile. "What'll you — I mean, gin, or Scotch, or —"

"Scotch. Whatever," I said. He nodded and poured me the drink. I sipped at it, trying to enjoy it, but soon Walt began to slip back into his fog of inaccessibility and I began to feel uncomfortable again.

Finally he looked in the direction of the bathroom. "Christ," he said softly. He shook his head, once, then stared down at the top of the bar.

"Wasn't your fault," I said in an undertone. "I'm sure she didn't —"

"I'm sure she did. She always does." He took a large swallow of his gin.

I fumbled for something to say. "Well, look — maybe she felt embarrassed after you came into the, uh, dining room. With the two of us like that. Maybe she still felt embarrassed, and that made her tense up, and snap at you like that."

"Yeah." I don't think I convinced him. "Shit, Jud, I hope you don't think I'm mad about that. I mean, I know how much of a thing you two had going before she married me. I guess that kind of thing doesn't die as easily as — others."

Marriages? I wondered. "It's not that, Walt."

He didn't hear me. "You were more her age in the first damn place," he said. "You should've married her, Jud. You spoke the same language."

"But different dialects. Would've never worked, Walt."

"And this has? So maybe you'd be starving in a garret somewhere, using diapers for canvas, how should I know? At least you wouldn't have been caught dead near any — goddamned nuke plant. . . ."

"Hey," I said, "c'mon, knock it off. You love that kind of work. Don't put it down just because —"

"Love doesn't mean shit these days," he said. "I'm a good nuts-and-bolts man, Jud, *you* know that; always have been. Remember all those wacky contraptions I used to build in the garage when we were kids? The firecracker factory, and you'd agent the stuff around the neighborhood?"

"Hell, yes. You almost blew up the whole damn block with that thing."

He chuckled. "Yeah. And the time the tornado almost did it for us, the blackout —"

"— and you made candles out of a couple of bottles of shaving lotion and some wicks —"

"Jesus, yes." He laughed. His laughter faded, and became a bitter smile. "But that's not where the money is, today. Nuts-and-bolts are a dime a gross. Theoretical men are the up-and-coming, and I — I've never been too good on theory."

The pleasant mood of nostalgia drew away like a soundless tide. I stared down at my drink, saw I hadn't had much, and quickly took a burning swallow.

He glanced again at the bathroom. "Christ," he repeated, turning back to me. "God damn it, Jud, I *do* wish you'd married Beck. You'd have given her a good life. I mean that. What have I given her? A full-time job and a millstone in the shape of a son. Christ — I wish . . ." He let the sentence trail off.

I stared at him, trying to understand the feeling I had for him now after so many years, the feeling different from the animal pity by the dinner table.

On impulse I said, "Are you hurting, Walt?"

His voice was tired. Dear God, was it tired.

"I hurt all the time, man," he said.

We didn't talk for a long time after that, not until Becky returned from the bathroom, but by then it was too late: I'd seen my brother in his eyes.

"Getting late, Becky," Mother said. "We should really give Jamie his presents now, before Judson has to go."

Becky sat splayed in a large, overstuffed chair; her body seemed to tighten like a watch wound to midnight, and there was an odd tone to her voice. "I'm sure Jud doesn't have to leave — quite so early, do you, Jud?"

"Well, I —"

"Open them now," Walt said, entering the living room with a large flat package tucked under his arm. "It'll give Jamie and Jud some time alone with the presents."

"Walter, you'll give away the surprise," Mother admonished him.

"Not if we open them now," he insisted, and plopped the package down on the coffee table in front of Jamie. He moved to Becky's side. "Jud, why don't you open it for Jamie?"

I went over and picked up the package. Out of the corner of my eye I saw Becky stand up, apparently trying to escape one more ritual, but Walt took her by the waist and held her close to him, proudly. Becky's face went pale, her facial muscles tightened Jamie-hard. Walt was beaming happily, perhaps attempting to forget the brief honesty he had shared with me.

"From both of us, Jamie," he said as I unwrapped the present: the large white sketch pad, the canvases, the tray of expensive watercolors, the thin brushes with stems as thick as Jamie's fingers.

"Hey, nice," I said, putting them on Jamie's lap. "Damned good canvas, Walt."

"Thanks. I looked for days to find the right kind. I was a little worried it wouldn't be."

I didn't doubt it; Walt's kindnesses were clumsy but sincere. Becky seemed unaffected, however — Walt's sweaty grip held her in a vise tangible only for her, visible only to me.

She broke away from him and walked quickly past Mother. "Why don't we get dessert ready, Mother, and let Jud show Jamie a little about the supplies?" Already heading toward the kitchen.

"I'll give you a hand," Walt said, following her. Becky slammed open the swinging kitchen doors with the flat of her hands; I felt a sudden upsurge of sympathy for her, a returning anger at Walt: *Leave her alone! Stop pawing her, making her one with you, this family!*

But that was ridiculous. She was already one with the family, or the cage that the family had become. Mother paused a moment as Walt disappeared into the kitchen, and then she followed him in.

I turned to Jamie. He was trying to open the oversized sketch pad with his undersized fingers. I crouched down to help him. "Here, Jamie, let me —"

His hands clenched suddenly into tight, angry fists. The effect was of two pale, fragile spiders abruptly turned compact and venomous. Startled — no, let me admit it: frightened — I drew back my own hands.

His fists unclenched, but the rigidity did not leave them; slowly, methodically, Jamie opened the sketch pad and allowed the large floppy cover to fall over his knees. He ran his left hand over the smooth bond surface while his right reached for a number two pencil. In one unbroken motion he began to sketch — to doodle — on the paper.

"Well," I said inanely, "maybe we should go over some of

the basic techniques. We don't have much time, I know, but — would you like that, Jamie?"

The pencil continued to scribble and between absent-minded doodles Jamie wrote *Yes* in the middle of the sheet.

"Okay, fine." The hands continued their random pattern across the paper. I watched them, fascinated, and tried to collect my thoughts; I spoke, hardly listening to what I was saying.

"The thing you have to remember," I said, "is that art is life and life is movement; we move, the world moves about us. The interface between the inner movement — us — and the outer movement — the world — is touch. Touch is very important in art. . . ."

(But how could anyone who would never move more than an inch at a time know of inner movement or outer movement or any interface between the two? Without movement, could there be touch, could there be sight?

(I made my art from that interface, the different touchings of environment and ego. But Jamie had *one* environment — unchanging save for tantalizing glimpses through books of a world outside, static, stale, dying; had it stunted his ego? What kind of dreams could he possibly paint?

(Only wet dreams that would never be more than that, only an aching need to move and be moved that would never be filled. Only — the family. Until they died and Jamie was put in a home, until then it would be only the four of them, trapped in a world without sky, turning year by year into figures from that faded yellow wallpaper. . . .

(As they had almost done to *me?*)

"Jamie," I said. He continued scribbling. "Jamie," my

voice low, my heart pounding, "I don't know if you can understand this, I don't know if I do, but —

"You can't let them define you, Jamie. Do you see? You can't let them make you into what they think you are. What they think you can be. They almost did it to me — Mother and Walt first, but Becky too, she wanted a steady dull man and she almost made me into another Walt. They almost did it, Jamie, that's the important thing — they *almost did it.*"

Jamie's pencil ran across the page, guided by seemingly absent fingers: *You escaped.*

I stared at the words and they seemed to lose their reality for me. "I hope so, Jamie. God, I hope so. But you can, too. You can! Just by being — what they don't expect. By being alive, God damn it."

Something stirred in his eyes. His hand-action became savage, rough.

Alive, he scrawled.

The pencil snapped between his fingers.

I turned away just as Becky and Mother and Walt reëntered the room with the birthday cake. Eleven candles burned with that same weak, flickering fire I had seen in all the eyes in this room. I felt off-balance as I stood up from my crouch.

"Happy birthday, Jamie," Mother said. "Walter, why don't you blow out the candles?"

"Sure," he said. "But hey, why don't we sing first? Hell, we haven't done that in years. Right, Beck? What the hell. Come on, Beck, let's sing."

I saw Becky's eyes go cold as frosted glass, and though I

could not read the thoughts behind their sudden opacity, looking at them I felt a lingering chill.

"We still have one present to open," Becky said tonelessly. "Excuse me, I'll get it." She went quickly into the bedroom. I tried to catch her attention with a glance, tried to telepathize my fear; *Don't do it, Back. Whatever it is, don't do it.*

Walt called out to her, his tone a bit hurt: "I thought we were giving a joint present, Beck. I mean, I thought it was from the two of us."

Becky (from the bedroom): "This isn't for Jamie."

Walt (puzzled): "It isn't?"

"No," and she reëntered with a small, fat package. "I've been thinking about giving it for a — long time now. . . . It's for you, Walter."

"Me?" The confusion in his voice was mixed with a dull, unquestioning pleasure. He couldn't detect the sharp edge of secrecy in Becky's voice, as I could; maybe that was one of the things she wanted from a husband. He took the box from her hands, his fingers fumbling with the wrapping. I looked only briefly into Becky's eyes before I had to glance away. I felt sick. I wanted to run. I wanted to escape.

"Hell, Becky, you really shouldn't have. . . ." He was touched, I could feel it as he threw off the last of the wrapping. He ripped off the lid of the box and his eager smile turned empty. His face turned that peculiar white that faces pale to before nausea. He looked up and stared at Becky as if she had shot him.

He dropped the box. A gun fell out, a .45 I think it was, its muzzle covered by a thin, taut piece of — *rubber*. . . .

"Actually quite functional," Becky was saying, and I wondered if she even heard herself; "used by French army officers during World War I — protection from mud, and rain, and —"

Walt clenched his hand into a fist. "Bitch," he whispered, over and over, "bitch, bitch, sweet *bitch* . . ."

Their choreography was perfect. She turned; he grabbed at her, missed; she ran into the bedroom, slamming the door shut, locking it, and then Walt was banging away at it, slamming the hard wood with raw knuckles, his raging pathetic voice carrying back to us in the living room. . . .

Mother's eyes were closed. I stared at her. "They'll kill each other," I said, a world away. "Mother, they'll kill each other."

She opened her eyes and shook her head. "No. They never do."

And then I turned to Jamie and knew that my words to him had been unnecessary, my fears of him groundless in themselves but seeds for new fears that I might nurture to full ripeness. Jamie was himself, no one else. Jamie was sitting quietly, listening to his parents' screams. Jamie was smiling.

We close with another tale of planetary exploration—but this time the explorers aren't human, and the world is Earth. It's a world that frightens these strange star-travelers, and as you read their descriptions of it you'll discover that fear can be compounded by being experienced through someone completely different from you.

Fritz Leiber is one of the most honored writers in the history of science fiction and fantasy; among his many Hugo and Nebula Awards were those for his novels *The Big Time* and *The Wanderer.*

The Eeriest Ruined Dawn World

Fritz Leiber

THE ASTROGATOR's Dear Friend asked, "But of all the worlds you found where awareness had budded and then destroyed itself — and there were more of them than I had realized! — which was the most interesting?"

"I can't tell you that, you cold-blooded fish!" the Astrogator replied. "They were all equally interesting . . . and equally sad." He paused. "But I can tell you which was the strangest — no, that's not the word."

"The eeriest," the Planetographer supplied.

"Yes, that describes it," the Robotist agreed, "provided you were both referring to the star we called Lonely and its planet Hope. I thought so! Yes, the eeriest."

"Oh, good!" the Robotist's Fond Companion urged. "I love spooky stories."

"Tales of death and desolation — by all means!" the Planetographer's Sweet Love chimed, smacking her lips.

"Morbid monster!" he told her playfully.

"Prurient parasite!" she joked back.

"Which of us should begin?" the Astrogator asked.

"You!" they all chorused: his two fellow explorers and the stay-at-home mates of all three of them were gathered together in convivial and truly symbiotic friendship for the first time since the three explorers' great voyaging.

The Astrogator finished his drink, was poured another, and began, "We surfaced from hyperspace out in the Arm. Our destination was a star in a tiny cluster, a star so small and somehow woebegone we called her Lonely."

"Out in the Arm!" his Dear Friend commented. "Then it was during the period when we were out of telepathic contact entirely. *Our* lonely time."

"That's right. As we approached her, we studied her planets. The Seventh was trebly ringed, quite a rarity. The Fifth was long since shattered, almost pulverized. An old deep nuclear suicide, or else a dual planet, inharmoniously paired. Analysis of data we recorded may still tell."

"Or perhaps (remotely possible) he encountered a small

dark wanderer passing through Lonely's space," the Planetographer put in.

"What a way to go!" his Sweet Love said. "Serve him right for playing around."

"No fault of his — he'd be a sitting duck."

"Who's telling this?" the Astrogator complained. "Now moving in closer to Lonely, we found her Third altogether ideal for life, right in the middle of the viable volume. And he was paired, with tides to stir his atmosphere and waters — no chance of stagnation. The secondary was quite small, had long ago died a natural death —"

"Perhaps," the Planetographer interjected.

The other continued without comment, "— but the primary was the right size with a rich atmosphere, so we named him Hope. And there were radiations patterned by intelligence coming from him. That seemed conclusive, and yet" — he paused — "and yet almost from the start there was something about him that seemed wrong."

He paused again. The Planetographer nodded and said, "His atmosphere was rich, all right — too rich in hydrocarbons to my taste."

The Robotist observed, "And as for those radiations indicating intelligence, well, there began to be a sameness about them, a lack of interplay, a lack of the day-to-day dynamisms characteristic of mental life in ferment."

"A time of cultural calm?" his Fond Companion suggested. "A quiet period?"

"We thought so for a while, my dear."

The Astrogator went on, "I put *Quester* into a parking orbit matching Three's natural period of rotation so that our ship hung above one meridian, shuttling north and south through an arc of about one-fourth of a circle as Three spun."

He looked toward the Planetographer across the table floating between them.

"Three showed at least three times as much ocean as land," the latter took up. "Our daily swing took us across two continents joined by a serpentine isthmus, from the east coast of the northern continent to the west coast of the southern near its tip, and back again. Three was, or had been, inhabited all right, and by beings of considerable if strange mentation, for we passed over numerous cities —"

"Cities? What are those?" the Astrogator's Dear Friend wanted to know.

"Abnormal concentrations of dwellings and other structures. Inorganic cancers. As I was saying — over numerous cities and great wide roads and paved flat fields that might have been for the mass celebration of religious rites, or else for the launching and landing of large winged vehicles. In fact, the inhabitants of Three seemed to have had a passion for sealing in the surfaces of their continents with various inorganic materials."

"How very strange," the Robotist's Fond Companion observed.

"Yes, indeed. At the north end of our daily swing there was an especially large concentration of cities — a cluster of inorganic boils, you might say — beside and in the ocean's edge. The one of these containing the most monstrous structures was a long narrow island surrounded by a mighty dike at least one-fourth the height of the tallest structures it guarded — and they were tall! — and against the top of which, or near, the dark, restless oceanic waters ceaselessly lapped and crashed. This city stood just off the continent. A very deep river led down to it from the north, while farther to the northwest lay five great, swollen lakes, half run together."

"Did he have ice caps? I mean Three, of course," the Planetographer's Sweet Love inquired sharply.

"No."

"But had he formerly?"

"My love, you are intuitive. Yes, he'd had ice caps until very recently, and they had melted, raising the ocean's level, and the dike had been built against that, stage by stage.

"But oh, the monstrousness of those buildings the dike guarded! — especially toward the south end of the island. Their height, immensity, and blocky shapes! But most particularly the way they were crowded together stiflingly like giant columns of prismatic basalt. With your own eyes or by telepathy you've all seen monuments on other planets, built by races that favor such oddities. Well, imagine them *without vistas*, jammed side to side, literally wall against wall, hundreds and hundreds of them, thousands and thousands — and many scores of them tall enough to peer over the dike at the illimitable, wind-fretted sea. Or think of planets heavily overpopulated, so that two skyscrapers actually approach each other as closely as the sum of their heights, and then imagine *them* packed together with no room between, the windows of their eyes blinded, the doors of their mouths screaming against solidity — as if space herself had been conquered by matter, as threatens in the hearts of some dwarf stars. I tell you, as we stared down through our instruments at that monstrous city, we wondered only why it had not squeezed itself out of existence — popped like a pressured seed out of the space-time fabric into chaos!"

"But just how high, really, was the dike?" his Sweet Love asked.

"A hundred times my height."

"So, ten times my length. Yes, that's pretty tall," she allowed, smiling at him beside her. The other four around the floating table nodded or otherwise expressed agreement.

The Planetographer continued, "The walled and narrow off-shore island city, although spectacular and with a macabre fascination all its own, did not monopolize our attention. We studied other cities along our swing — in fact, all the sea and land we passed over. We set up two observation satellites in other orbits along other meridians. We sent down probes to sample the atmosphere and waters. We pinpointed the sources of Three's radiation and further analyzed it. By every means we knew, we looked for life.

"Gradually it was borne in on us (and to our considerable astonishment since we'd seen the cities) that our first horrible suspicion was correct. Hope (Three) was dead — as sterile as an asteroid in intergalactic space, or baking as it orbits a star just outside her corona. By their unbridled industrial and technological development, Three's inhabitants had doomed and destroyed all life there, even the monocellular and the viral. The atmosphere was lethal. The great oceans were poison."

"And the patterned radiations," the Robotist put in, "were being broadcast by automatic, self-repairing instruments that would continue to do so until their sun-power failed. Mere echoes of intelligence long since dead."

There was a general silence.

The Planetographer resumed, elegiacally, "The ruined dawn worlds are all sad, a hundred self-destroyed for every one that manages to cope with the first great crisis of intelligence: environment's control, ecology. Sad, sad to see a planet blasted by nuclear warfare, perhaps riven to its very core. But such deaths at least are swift and sudden. Saddest of all to see a planet like Hope, dead of slow poison, where even his intelligent inhabitants became, by overpopulation, only one more pollutant. To think of his vigorous peoples creating and building, entertaining all sorts of romantic and grandiose plans for the future, believing themselves in control of their lives, when all the while they were only quietly digging their own graves, planning their deaths, building their monstrous tombs, patiently elaborating the venoms that would carry them off — and all local life with them. For life was gone on Hope, totally gone."

There was, as it were, a collective sigh from the three stay-at-homes around the floating table.

"But then," the Planetographer said dramatically, "there came the event that appeared to refute that seemingly irrevocable conclusion. Out of the cenotaph of the monstrous diked island city there rose a fiery plumed rocket aimed at us. We let it approach for a space, then mastered it with repulsor and tractor beams and, when its fuel burned out, placed it in the same orbit as *Quester* at a safe distance. Robot examination — but that's the field of my friend across the table."

"— Showed it to be a fission-fusion missile of some potency," the Robotist took up. "It was the *delay* in the firing of the missile that seemed to argue *against* a merely automatic defense system triggered by the approach of *Quester* and *for* the presence of living intelligence. If it were merely a robot system like the sun-powered broadcasters, with the decision arrived at by computers, why the delay? Of course there were alternate explanations, such as a cumulative stimulus being required to work the trigger. Still, as I sent down the probes that would engage in detailed explorations, inside structures as well as out, far underground if need be, I felt more than usual excitement, even an uneasy anticipation, as to exactly what they would discover.

"As you know, the probes are of several different sorts, ranging from spheroidal floaters to true robots with eight legs, about my size, able to walk and climb, open or cut through doors, and also fire grapnel lines to bridge gaps, et cetera.

"Such probes were sent not only into the diked city, but also to other localities: on the two serpent-linked continents, on a larger cluster of continents on Three's other side, and on one lonely land mass at his southern pole.

"The same quite interesting general finding soon came back from many localities. The larger structures everywhere were quite devoid of the remains of Three's intelligent life form, which later turned out to be a biped bibrach with an internal mineral skeleton. Its sensorium and organs of mentation were carried precariously in an external braincase, instead of within a sturdy cephalothorax, such as ours, or a single streamlined body, such as yours, my dears."

"How very odd," his Fond Companion said.

"A mineral endoskeleton instead of pliant cartilage," the Planetographer's Sweet Love observed with some distaste. "Bones on the inside, ugh!"

"And how much nicer to be born with tentacles, like ours, or a neat and protective leathery exoskeleton, like yours," the Astrogator's Dear Friend said to him.

"The biped bibrachs had tentacles of a sort," he told her. "Five on each limb, with little bones inside."

"Sounds much too stiff. They must have moved about like rheumatic demi-octopuses. Or paraplegic arachnoids, for that matter."

"As I was saying," the Robotist cut short the digression, "although we found numerous bibrach skeletons, there were none within the larger structures — no, these were empty except for large stores of video and audio records — which did not clash with the notion that these places were for the celebration of rare and arcane religious rites, holy and occult buildings. Why, several of them near the center of the cluster of continents on Three's other side were shaped like huge pyramids and almost solid — just a few tiny rooms and passageways deep inside. Another, which stood on a peninsula one-fifth of our swing down the diked city's meridian, was a hollow cube so vast that several of the bibrachs' smaller winged vehicles could have been flown about inside.

"But as you'd expect, the structures in the diked island city were the most monstrous, though one at the drowned foot of the fourth western lake was taller. A large number of our probes were busy there — many of them exploring underground, for the island was formed entirely of a fine-grained rock, which the bibrachs had honeycombed with tunnels and basements under basements, like inverted buildings — towers and downward-pointing pinnacles of space inside solidity.

"And then from the probe that had gone deepest — as deep below the surface as the tallest tower extended above — a message was relayed back: it had found life."

There was an uneasy stirring around the round table. It almost communicated itself to the water in which the six friends floated.

"We asked our probes for details and to a degree we got them, although the distance was too great, the angles too sharp, and the relays too many for the accurate transmission back of pictures. There was *one* source of life-indications only, *one* being, and it was strangely wedded to the inorganic."

"Horrors! But how?" his Fond Companion demanded.

"That is the thing our robots could not tell us. We were consumed with wonder and with dread, but above all with a burning curiosity. We decided to go down and see for ourselves — all three, since none of us would consent to be left behind."

"But that was fantastically dangerous," she protested, "and quite against all sound exploratory practice."

"When we are out in the wild worlds of the Rim," the Astrogator put in, "we are not always so particular. I'm afraid we take chances."

"Especially when we are also out of telepathic range," the Planetographer added.

"Besides, there was this *drive*, this burning urge," the

Robotist continued. "As soon as the *Quester* had swung farthest north, we suited up and took the landing craft down.

"The skies were brownish gray when at last we saw them from below. So were the seas storming around the island. We landed in a narrow gorge — slit, rather — at the base of two vast rectilinear pylons, from deep below which the signs of life were coming.

"We disembarked, feeling claustrophobic and unclean, despite the sure protection afforded by our suits. The pavement was less littered than I'd expected, though I did note the braincase of a bibrach, brown as the ribbon of sky overhead. The structures hemming us in, their windowed walls staring shortsightedly at each other, were indescribably oppressive.

"The cramping gorge ended at the great dike, and even as I looked up, up, up at its top, I saw a cloud of brown spray thrown high above it as a great wave broke against its other side. The thought of all that poisoned water pressing in on us from all sides, and we already far below its surface, added to the dark weight upon my feelings.

"Our robots were waiting for us, and with them we began the subterranean stage of our journey. We descended chiefly by a series of narrow, vertical, square-sectioned shafts bored in the rock. These carried boxlike vehicles, but we preferred to drop by our own lines. I will not dwell on my ever increasing feeling of oppression. Suffice it that the rocks' vast mass was added in my thoughts to that of the waters.

"We entered at last a dim world of computers, the inorganic remnant, mindlessly functioning, of the core of the bibrachs' culture. At its nadir we found our robots clustered around a deep-set window. Here, we knew, was the life they'd found. We ordered them aside and looked through ourselves and saw a life-support system automatically maintaining a single bibrach brain that was cyborged to the computer around it."

"Cyborged — how very dreadful," his Fond Companion breathed. "The marriage of flesh to metal — abomination."

"For a long while we stood staring at that poor pinkish thing. The same thoughts and feelings were building up in all three of our minds: the loneliness and agony and desolation of that captive mind, last of its race, sundered by light-years (at least until our arrival) from any other known mentality — the mind that at some pinnacle of hate or terror had sent the rocket at us, the mind that might die the next moment, or perhaps live for eons. In the end I found myself thinking just this one thought: that if Death has a brain anywhere in the universe, it is there on Hope (that circles Lonely way out in the Arm), deep in the rock of the diked island city.

"Perhaps (you'll say) we should have tried to communicate with it, even to disentangle it at any risk from its environs. I only know we didn't. Instead we returned (fled would be more honest), up the skinny shafts into the brown day of the monstrous city, and embarked to chase the *Quester* down its meridian without a thought of waiting its return. Once aboard, we picked up all our probes and left (fled!) Hope and all of Lonely's planetary system and didn't feel really safe until we were in hyperspace again."

"Think of the loneliness of that last brain . . ." the Planetographer murmured.

"That was the eeriest ruined dawn world — just as I told you at the start," the Astrogator said with conviction. "Don't you agree, my love?"

"I think all three of you behaved like a pack of lunatics," his Dear Friend answered. "You're not to be trusted, any of you, outside the range of our telepathy."

"Why didn't you stay and at least try to talk to that buried brain?" the Planetographer's Sweet Love demanded.

"We had this feeling —" he began, then shrugged.

"We were *scared*," the Robotist said.

"Well, it's been nice to get together," his Fond Companion said briskly, "but now it's time we broke up. You and I, my dear, have to check out that terrarium we're buying at Deep Six."

And without further ceremony the three arachnoids, about as large as gorillas but with brains larger than man's and hands even more manipulative, scrambled into the shoulder niches of their ichthyoid partners. The latter, who were the size of long, sinuous whales with brains one-fifth their mass, supported by ocean and great webs of cartilage, arched upward and then dove down with ponderous grace. Now the ocean was empty again except for the abandoned table bobbing and rocking in the wake of that great treble sounding.

Beware the future; it is the great unknown. As inevitable as it is uncertain in its manifestations, the future brings dreams — and horrors — to light. One day the unimaginable will become as real and tangible as the glint of laboratory steel, a cold, inhuman breath at the back of the neck, the mutant stare of a child who can no longer smile.

Each of the nine science fiction writers whose new and original stories appear in this volume has a uniquely terrifying vision of what may lie before us in time and space. Guesswork? Perhaps. But science fiction has never been simply pure amusement. It *has* been prophecy. So consider *The Ides of Tomorrow* a set of prophecies, if you like, and pray they don't come true.

Brian Aldiss, a British writer, is a winner of both the Hugo and the Nebula awards, author of many stories and a dozen books. His titles include *The Long Afternoon of Earth* and a critical history of SF entitled *Billion Year Spree*.

Robert Bloch first became known as the author of *Psycho*. In a career that spans forty years, he has won many fans with his outrageous sense of humor. One of his best-known works is "That Hell-Bound Train," a Hugo Award winner.

Alan Brennert, a graduate of the Clarion workshop, is considered one of the most promising new writers of science fiction. His first story was published in 1973.

Harlan Ellison has earned a major literary reputation, and many awards, in almost every medium. He was the originator of the influential Dangerous Vision Series, has won five